# Plum Crazzzy

## By
## Monique Jewell Anderson

Literally Speaking Publishing House
Washington, DC
www.LiterallySpeaking.com

2020 Pennsylvania Avenue, NW, #406
Washington, DC 20006
Visit our website at
www.LiterallySpeaking.com

Copyright © 2004 by Monique Jewell Anderson
ISBN: 1-929642-07-5
Published by Literally Speaking Publishing House

LSPH trade cloth printing 2004, Printed in the U.S.A.,
First Printing 10 9 8 7 6 5 4 3 2 1

Literally Speaking Publishing House, one of America's fastest growing publishers of adult fiction and nonfiction hardcover as well as trade paperback books, is the publisher of several national bestsellers including *Blessed Assurance, Chocolate Thoughts* and *Mocha Love*.

With its upcoming titles, *Plum Crazzzy, Illusions, Nowhere To Turn, Don't Mess With Me, Journey to the Light, Forbidden Fruit, Preachers' Row* and *Speak to My Heart*, LSPH is dramatically expanding its diverse mixture of first-time and veteran authors who uniquely capture life's joys and pains, fears and hopes, pitfalls and successes through refreshing characters, creative story lines, and inspirational writing.

With its bold, refreshingly original and inspirational books, LSPH is becoming known throughout the nation as the home of "Writing that Speaks To You"—Writing that speaks to your experiences, dreams, desires, mind and most importantly, your heart. Welcome to the LSPH experience.

www.LiterallySpeaking.com

# DEDICATION

In a church service about twelve years ago, I sat by a woman who I didn't know. Then the pastor at the time instructed us to pray for our neighbor. So we both turned to each other and I began to pray. But the entire time I prayed, I really felt inside that I had nothing to offer God. After the woman prayed for me, she sat down, pulled out a piece of paper, and wrote the following words to me. "The Lord God said, 'There's more of Me in you, than you think you know. There's more of Me in you, than you realize.' Amen."

This book is dedicated to all people who think they have nothing to offer God. May you never feel or think that way EVER again.

This book and my life are dedicated to God for His unfailing love and belief in me! I move on, I live because God has seen my ending before my beginning. I will forever be grateful to God for choosing to use me. For I am truly not the author, HE IS. He just allowed me to put my name to it. May God forever be Glorified and Lifted Up.

Old Testament:

Psalms 27:4  One thing have I desired of the LORD, that will I seek after; that I may dwell in the house of the LORD all the days of my life, to behold the beauty of the LORD, and to inquire in His temple.

New Testament:

Romans 8:28  And we know that all things work together for good to them that love God, to them who are the called according to His purpose.

# ACKNOWLEDGMENT

To My Husband, Frank: Bone of my bone, flesh of my flesh. I used God's WORD because He said only His WORD will last forever. And when I think of you, I always think of Forever! Thank you for giving me the sweetest gift, all of YOU!

To My Children: Elise, Robert, Frankie, Brianna and Ahmore. I am so Godly proud of each of you. You make me who I am, and you sho' keep a momma grounded in what really matters!

To My Parents, Robert and Darlene Jewell; my sisters, Daiquiri and Derricka; and the rest of the family; Thank you for your unconditional love, support, hugs and so much laughter. My heart says, "I love you."

Felicia: You saw me through the eyes of God and not that of man. Instead of judging me, you loved me. Instead of pointing a finger, you kneeled in prayer. Instead of talking about me, you showed me through actions what a real woman of God is to be. Our hearts will forever be knitted together.

Linda: Real. Powerful. Bold. A true and loyal Friend, Sister.

I acknowledge and am deeply grateful for the men and women who have prayed me through! Who have loved me with God's love and who have embraced me with God's sweet touch. You all know who you are!

To the LSPH Family:

Executive Editor, Mychelle Morgan; Senior Editor, Jill Peddycord; Associate Editor, Marie Carter; Contributing Editors, Paul Morgan and Rachael Couch. You all didn't just edit a book, you listened and sought God in doing so. Your labor has not been in vain and I Thank You.

LSPH executives Maurice Calhoun, Shaun Stevenson, Paul Morgan, Lora Brown and Paul Robinson: you have my deep, sincere appreciation for your key leadership at critical junctures in this project.

Rod Dennis of Colabours Communication, without even saying one word to you directly, you captured on the cover what I envisioned my writing to convey. Pure genius.

To my fellow LSPH Authors: S. James Guitard: A man of integrity, a man of the WORD. Whatever you desire, the Lord says, "It is already done." Thank you for being willing and obedient. And to J.M. Branch, Jason Harley, Rebecca Simms and Angela Russell, do your thing and let's represent the King well.

A Very Special THANK YOU to:

Victoria Christopher Murray: The true pioneer in Christian Fiction. Thank you for stirring up the gift in me like no other, and for your insistent words of purpose and destiny over my life. You believed before I did. Seven years ago we made a promise to each other (you know what it was) and I just want you to know, from the core of my being, I'm grateful to God for your loyal friendship. You never forgot about me! Ever! I LOVE YOU, VICTORIA.

Jacquelin Thomas and Kim Roby: Christian authors who are not only making a difference in the lives of others, but who most importantly live what they believe. Thank you for leading the way in honor, integrity, sisterhood and in the love of Christ, our Savior.

To the countless readers, book clubs, bookstores and distributors, past, present and future, I look forward with great anticipation to meeting you on the road. We are going to have a ball!

# Plum Crazzzy

## By
## Monique Jewell Anderson

*"If you want to stop attracting dogs, you must first change your scent."*

**CHAPTER ONE**

I always wonder why am I the one who continually attracts the misfit man, the dog, if you will. At this point in my life and with all that I have to give, one nagging question remains: Why am I not in a committed relationship with a man who has more than just words to offer, but is a man of his word as well as most importantly a man of the WORD? Instead, I'm constantly ending up with a man with all types of needs but who is incapable of meeting any of mine. A man who wants love, but really has no idea of what love is. A man, who it turns out, wants a mother instead of a soul mate. Everything in me wants a man like my Father in heaven told me I should have. Loving. Dedicated. Sincere. Masculine. A real MAN.

A man like …

I first saw Mark at the new members' class. From the moment the associate pastor conducting the meeting said, "Come in," a hush fell over the room as all eyes and attention went immediately to the brown door. Mark stood six-foot-three and approximately two hundred fifteen pounds with long, chiseled arms that reflected long hours in the gym. His smooth demeanor and animal magnetism filled the room even before he fully entered it. His presence was undeniable and unmistakably real and raw. A quick glance around the conference room table let me know that many of the women just like me were being touched, and this time it wasn't by the Holy Spirit. Mark was driving us all crazy. My eyes focused on his lips, which were full like clouds, delicious and wet like my favorite ice cream, Black Walnut, on a hot summer's day. I watched him as he leaned further into the classroom and politely waved the minister over to him before he spoke to our class. I don't know what he actually said because my ears stopped listening just like my heart stopped beating. It was as if I had been transported into a Chinese movie where the lips don't quite match up with the words you hear. Then, and to my dismay, the door closed, and he faded out of my sight.

~~~~~~~~~

The night I met Mark I had on my favorite designer dress appropriately accessorized with a newly-acquired purse and matching shoes. My revealing short skirt, while very attractive, made me feel a little self-conscious in church, but I got over it faster than the several pairs of eyes that kept looking at it. However, my attire was purposeful in nature. Right after church I had another meeting with my ex-husband, Darren, and I *had* to be looking good. The only snag to my attitude was the snag in my stockings due to a splinter from an old wooden church pew. After the conclusion of the new members' class, I walked down the long, red-carpeted aisle trying to remember where the ladies' room was located. I had to check my face before seeing Darren. While fumbling in my purse for my makeup case, I heard a sound as though straight out of heaven. The voice rolled like thunder in a spring storm, but only softer and gentler.

"Excuse me, Miss," he said.

Tiptoeing like a graceful ballerina, I swirled around in slow motion. It was HIM. I hoped and prayed silently, "Please, Lord. Please, Lord. Don't let me look as stupid as I feel."

With his hand outstretched, he introduced himself. "Hi. I'm Mark. Mark Hayes. You look a little lost. Are you new here? Can I help you in some way?"

I tried desperately to release my frozen fingers from my makeup case in order to grasp hold of his hand. My hand pulled out of my purse just in time to meet the warmth of his. When he looked at me with those penetrating eyes, it reignited a fire deep within me that I knew had long ago been extinguished. His firm, round shoulders complemented a nicely tailored, navy blue pin-striped suit. Even through his clothes, I could visualize a flat washboard stomach. And those legs, they looked like vice grips, and I yearned to be the object between them. And his feet, well, all I can tell you is that I hoped the myth was true.

The multicolored, stained glass windows right behind him reminded me that I was still in church. I tried to quickly swallow the saliva that had built up in my mouth. Swallowing hard, I just knew my voice was gone or it would crack when I said my name. After what felt like an eternity, I finally said (in my usual hoarse, but sexy voice), "Hi, I'm Moniqué. I just attended the new members' class."

Mark replied, "Welcome."

I didn't want to seem rude, but I had a pressing meeting with Darren and still needed to pick up a new pair of stockings. So as politely as I knew how to sound, I said, "Thank you, it's great to be here," and reluctantly began making my way to the exit door and away from the man who, for that brief moment, made me forget all about my past.

As we approached the double-doors marked "Exit," I saw him increase his pace to reach the door before me. He smiled, pushed it open and said, "Have a good evening." The big, sunny smile I gave him was greeted by drizzling rain. I didn't want to get my hair wet, especially after the hours I had spent getting it right this morning. Mark read my facial expression and asked the gentleman next to us if he could borrow his umbrella and then offered to accompany me to my car (could things get any better? I don't think so), and of course, I accepted. We stopped midway and began to talk. In the middle of one of my sentences, Mark interrupted me and commented, "You are certainly one beautiful looking woman."

I'm sure I blushed right there on the spot. Thank goodness it was dark outside so he couldn't see it. Then he asked, "Would it be possible to exchange telephone numbers so I can keep in touch with you?" Lord knows I couldn't get my PDA out of my purse fast enough.

If women were moths, then Mark would have to be the red-hot flame, and I was willing to be burned to find out if he was the real deal. Like most women, I desire passion, excitement and danger. Admittedly so, I have fantasized about being pushed to the edge of my limits and then imagined being daringly rescued by my hero. Unfortunately, as experience has taught me, I normally just get pushed. But this time would be different.

After exchanging numbers, Mark said, "Have a good night. It was a pleasure meeting you, and I hope to talk to you real soon."

I nodded my head and smiled in agreement. I then slid into my car as he closed the car door. After waving at Mark one last time, putting on the car blinkers and carefully pulling out of a tight parking space, I thought about how gentleman-like it was for him to walk me to my car with an umbrella. Not a single drop of rain had touched my hair or my beautiful outfit, but that didn't mean I wasn't wet.

Driving to the club to meet Darren, my thoughts traveled back to the place I had just left. I don't know why, but for some strange reason I began to go back there, to church. I suppose, with all of the drama I had been through, I naturally gravitated back to what was most familiar to me. I also knew that something had to change in my life, and church and a real relationship with God would be a good place to start. I didn't go every Sunday, but compared to the last three years or so, it was more than usual. And I knew that once my praying mother found out, she would be jumping and shouting throughout the church. 'Cause back in the day, we were always there. I remember we went to a neighborhood church not too far from our middle class, two-story, red brick house. I think Momma must have liked the middle-of-the-week services best because the majority of my memories come from a Bible study or a testimony-type service. Daddy worked two jobs and was gone most nights. But that didn't stop Momma from going to church; in fact, we were usually the first ones there. Well, that was if you didn't count the gray-haired deacon who sat on the first pew, which made a loud crackling sound each time someone moved left or right. The deacon sat stiff as a board, moaned and sang some old, old spiritual.

"Mmm, mmm, mmm
What a Friend we have in Jesus, all our sins and griefs to bear!
What a privilege to carry everything to God in prayer!..."

As the night services continued way past our bedtimes, Momma often reached out and cradled in her arms whichever of her three little girls was the closest. Stephanie was the oldest.

Then there was me, Moniqué, and then the baby girl, Regina. It was usually me, though, who pushed and shoved my sisters out of the way in order to sit by Momma. I longed to be close to her, to smell her. Momma always smelled like lavender in the springtime. I remember how she cried softly during some services. Sometimes Momma sat slowly moving from side to side as she listened intently to a saint share a Scripture or testimony. Whatever was said on those nights, I could tell if Momma agreed with it or not just by watching her body language. If Momma moaned a little bit, it meant she thought the preacher was on the right track. If she moaned while swaying a little side to side with an occasional nodding of her head, that meant she personally connected with the sermon. But, if she moaned, nodded her head, and patted her feet while simultaneously waving one hand and clutching her Bible all at the same time, that definitely meant the gospel of Jesus was being preached, souls were on their way to being saved, and the devil was going to be mad as hell.

After years of my not going to worship services and months of church hopping, I was really starting to get into this church thing. I had even finally found my very own church home. What I didn't have, though, was a Bible. So, soon after joining church I decided to buy one, and boy, was that a trip and a half. There was so much to consider. Price. Style. Shape. Size. Color. And then, the translation or wording of the Bible. I spent less time picking out my wedding dress than I did trying to make the right Bible choice. I didn't know whether to get the King James Bible (whoever he is), the New International Version (I suppose this is a Bible for the world), The Living Bible (your guess is as good as mine) or I could have chosen The New Revised Standard Version (only God Himself knows about this one). Well, after about three hours in the store, I bought what everyone else in America primarily has, the King James Version, but mine had the bold print and tabs. You know I had to have the tabs. In a service, it usually took me anywhere from two to five full minutes just to locate a particular book in the Bible, and then I had to find the chapter and verse. By the time I found the Scripture, the minister was often finished reading it and halfway into his sermon. Talk about frustrating.

After purchasing my Bible, I was so excited that I wouldn't even let the sales clerk put it in a plastic bag. She offered to, but I told her no. I wanted to hold my Bible, to caress it like a newborn baby. The edges of the Bible pages were trimmed in sparkling gold and were crisp like new dollar bills. Because of its classy look, I was drawn to the leather edition. The outside of the Bible was pitch black and coated with a shiny gloss. The cover felt soft but sturdy to the touch. Right in the center of the Bible lay a cross, etched in the same sparkling gold. On the inside cover was a place to write your name and the date. I hesitated at first. This was God's Word, not just any ordinary book. But then, I wrote my name and the date in my best handwriting. At that moment, I knew that I was serious about church and the Word of God for the first time in my life.

~~~~~~~~~

After a long, deep breath, I got out of my car and walked across the club's packed parking lot. Darren purposely picked the meeting place because he was being spiteful. He knew I had rejoined church and was trying to put my partying days behind me. As soon as I stepped foot inside the lobby of the Royal, Darren stood to his feet. Then again, he was so short; the trip up was a quick one.

"Why are you frowning?" Darren asked as he entered my two feet of private space.

"I'm frowning?" I responded, unaware of my facial expression.

"Yeah, something wrong?"

"No. I'm okay. Are you ready to talk?" I asked like I had somewhere else to be.

"Yeah, I'm ready. Do you want to get a drink first?" Darren pointed to the bar.

The Royal used to be our spot. Actually, that's where we met, right out of high school. He was so smooth back then. And boy, did he have his stuff together. At least, that's what I thought at the age of eighteen. Then, Darren was twenty-two and on his own. I looked around the club for familiar faces but saw none. Something on the inside of me, though, still felt familiar as I remembered the good old days. We used to rock that spot. Me, Darren and a few friends of ours drank and danced all we could in one night. The thought of the sweet and tangy taste of an Amaretto Sour made my tongue salivate.

"Now you know I just left church."

"In that?" Darren stepped back and perused my outfit.

I tightened my blouse as if a button was loose. Then looking downward, the bulk of my thighs protruding out of my tight skirt, I said, "Yeah, in this. What's wrong with what I have on?"

He lifted both of his hands as if he had just touched something hot. Darren replied, "Nothing, my bad. Just asked a question is all. So, you want that drink or what?"

I had a choice. My mouth watered again. But my heart made

my tongue answer, "No, let's just go over to the quiet side so we can talk about the kids. That is why you called me over here, right?"

I led the way, and Darren followed closely behind me.

"Mo, you still got it going on. I forgot how good you look from behind."

"Darren. I didn't come here so you could stare at my anatomy." I quickly sat down at a table. Unconsciously, I tapped my foot and grooved to the beat of the song that played in the background. It was oldies but goodies night at the Royal, and they were jamming. Frankie Beverly & Maze were singing, "Before I Let Go." Darren saw me swaying to the beat.

"Do you wanna dance?" he asked.

"No. Why would you ask me that?" I straightened up in my seat.

"I see you over there. I know how much you love Maze."

Darren grinned that all too familiar, charming smile. It was *that* smile that got him into my pants so easily years ago. I felt myself weakening from the surroundings. Just as I was about to lean in Darren's direction, a waiter came over.

"Can I get you two something from the bar?"

My throat was drier than usual. A list of my favorite drinks ran through my mind. White Zinfandel. Long Island Ice Tea. Sex on the Beach.

Darren ordered for both of us, "Yes. The lady will have a White Zinfandel, and I'll have another Heineken."

The waiter turned to walk away.

"Excuse me. I need to change that please."

"Yes?"

"Change that Zinfandel to a Ginger Ale."

19

Darren and the waiter both said at the same time, "A Ginger Ale?"

I answered them both, "A Ginger Ale."

"Are you sick or are you trying to change on a brother or what?"

"I'm trying to change, period. Not for you or anybody else," I said as I tried to quench my thirst of the past with the ginger ale of the present, which the waiter had placed on the table.

"So, how are my babies doing? Do they need anything?" Darren began to reach into his pocket.

"They're great. And no, they don't need anything, but thanks for asking."

He put his hands back on the table.

"And school, how are they doing in school?"

"Nicole just got an award in Math, and Jordan just had his first basketball game on Saturday. Darren, you could have asked me all of this over the telephone. What was so important that you had to see me face to face?" My guard was up because Darren wasn't usually that cordial or talkative, at least not to me. I attributed his demeanor to the drink he had in his hand and to the ones he probably consumed prior to me meeting him.

"Always the direct one, huh. You can't ever just enjoy the moment. Gotta be in control all the time," Darren said as he lifted his Heineken to his lips and rolled his dark brown eyes at me.

The air was thick with tension as we both sat across the table from one another. All of a sudden, the music stopped.

I leaned back in my chair, folded my arms and silently prayed, "Please, Lord, not this mess again."

Darren put his empty beer bottle on the table and put his hand back in his pocket. He threw a crisp twenty-dollar bill in the center of the table and walked away.

"Darren," I called to him, but he didn't answer.

~~~~~~~~

I went straight to Stephanie's to pick up my babies.

"Hey, everybody," I shouted, opening the door without knocking.

"Momma," Nicole said, as Jordan jumped off the couch, ran over to me and gave my legs a big hug.

"Did you miss Momma, Jordan?" I said bending down and hugging him back.

"Yeah, Momma," he said while blushing.

"Girl, you know that boy can't go five minutes without his momma."

Jordan let go of my legs, turned around, and faced his uncle. "Uncle Larrieeee," Jordan whined.

"Larry. Where's Steph?" I asked.

"Upstairs," Larry answered without taking his eyes off the basketball game.

"Be right back, y'all," I yelled as I jumped the stairs two at a time.

Stephanie was in her bathroom. I rushed right in (disregarding the stench, or what I call funk). I showed her Mark's telephone number.

She looked up at me and said, "What? I thought you went to church, not the club."

"I did go to church," and with my hand over my mouth I said, "and to the club."

"Okay, I knew about your meeting at church, but how did

you manage to go to the club?"

"I had to meet Darren."

Stephanie's eyebrows raised as she spoke, "So. How did. That go?"

I smacked my lips and rolled my eyes.

"Shoot, let's talk about him later. Let's get back to the telephone number."

"Stephanie Clark-Thomas!" I said, surprised.

"What? If I can't have the life I really want, I might as well live out my fantasy through you."

Stephanie thought my life was the epitome of womanhood in the twenty-first century. She envied my single-parent lifestyle. If Stephanie could tell it, her seven years as a wife and the mother of two children were boring and unfulfilling. My life, on the other hand, was off the chain according to her. Stephanie used to say to me, "At least you can come and go as you please. You don't have to answer to nobody but God. Your money is your own," and so on and so on. Stephanie didn't understand or grasp the real picture, though. Sure, it was nice to come and go as I pleased. And for the most part, she was right on every front. However, Stephanie didn't go home with me every night to an empty bed. When she turned over at night, there was a loving husband and warm body next to her. She had someone to share her hopes and dreams with. I didn't. So, every time Stephanie started in with me about my so-called I-have-it-made life, I told her, "The grass always looks greener while you are on the other side. But wait until you get the water bill."

Of course, I had to sit down (yes, in the bathroom) and tell her the whole story about how Mark and I met. But first, I had to fill her in on the details of my meeting with Darren. Stephanie was concerned. Having a big sister to talk to was comforting.

Steph and I moved our conversation out of the bathroom and onto her queen-sized bed. We must have talked a long time because the next thing we knew, Larry had taken off his clothes (in the bathroom) and gotten into bed. Steph looked at me and winked. Without a word, I leaned over and gave her a kiss on the cheek. Winking back at her, I began to walk back downstairs as she called out to me.

"Nee," Stephanie said as she placed her hand on her tummy, "How are you feeling?"

With my head lowered, I halfway smiled and said, "I'm okay. Thank you for asking, for caring." I didn't know how she did it, but she always remembered that day.

After arriving home and placing my purse on my small kitchen table, I took off my heels in the hallway and went straight to my bedroom. I pounced on the bed, grabbed the remote and turned on the TV. *Alias* was on, and Sydney was kicking butt. Nicole and Jordan had already put on their pajamas, said their prayers and gone to sleep. They knew the drill without me having to say a word. Jordan must have been really tired because he usually tried to sneak or bribe his way into my bed with a kiss. But not this night.

With a quick turn of the front door doorknob, I made sure it was locked; I then made one final check on the kids. Jordan was in his usual position, snuggled up against the wall, while Nicole slept so close to the edge of the bed, it was a miracle that she didn't roll over, fall and bust her head. Kissing them both on their lips, I went into my bathroom and took a shower. Afterwards, I put on my favorite T-shirt and got down on my knees by the bed. Just as I finished my prayers, the phone rang.

"Who in the world," I thought, "could this be?" I looked at the digital clock which sat on my nightstand. It read 11:30 p.m. I answered the phone.

The person on the other end of the line waited until I said, "Hello," a couple of times before they hung up. I read the caller ID box, "Unavailable." I hated when it said that. The phone rang again, and I snatched it before it rang twice.

"Hell...o," I said with an attitude.

"Hi, it's Mark. We met tonight at church."

I had to regroup for a second; then I was flattered. Old boy wasted no time, did he?

"I hope I caught you before you went to bed."

"I'm not asleep," I answered as I tried to get the tiredness out of my throat.

"So, did you enjoy your meeting tonight?" Mark asked.

"I did. It was interesting."

"Now that you're a member, I'll get to see your pretty face more often. I saw you sitting in the back of the church before the meeting began tonight, and I wanted to get a closer look at you. That's why I interrupted you all," Mark admitted.

"Oh really?" Pausing for a moment, I said, "So, how long have you been going to New Life Baptist?" I tried to change the subject because I was slightly embarrassed that he actually interrupted a meeting just to see me.

"All of my life."

"Aren't you a deacon or something in the church? I thought I heard someone in the meeting tonight refer to you as one?"

"Yeah, I am," Mark said. He sounded reluctant to talk about that aspect of his life. His voice dropped a notch in tone in response to my question.

I felt a little bit uneasy, so I changed the subject again.

"So, tell me something about yourself, other than your being a deacon of the church."

"I'd love to. Over dinner maybe?" He paused. "Are you free tomorrow night?"

"Sure," I said without a thought to any plans I might have had.

"Oh, Moniqué, I am so sorry. I can't tomorrow. Please accept my apology. I forgot I have another meeting I need to attend."

"Sounds like you have meetings quite often," I responded.

"Yeah, most nights. But I can be persuaded...."

Although Mark and I didn't meet the next night, we did eventually hook up on isolated occasions. We did like most couples do, go to the movies and out to dinner. Our conversations were easygoing and simple. I did most of the talking, opening up, whereas Mark was a little reserved, especially on the subject of him being a deacon. Mark was adamant about keeping his private life just that, private. He never mixed his private life as a man with his duties as a deacon. He said he didn't like to talk about the responsibilities and pressures of "shop." I thought it was a bit strange at first, but he was able to convince me over time. Made sense to me; I wasn't a deacon nor did I know what deacons did, so I didn't push.

How could I? I was a single woman rearing two kids alone. I knew about responsibilities and pressure very well. It was hard squeezing time in for a phone call, let alone an actual date. No matter how much time we really wanted to spend together, our dating had to be coordinated well in advance, if at all.

After canceling the last three dates in a row because of the kids, the job or whatever, I invited Mark over to my place for a special dinner on the weekend the kids went to Darren's. I wanted to show him how much I appreciated his patience and understanding each time I canceled. I found those qualities in him very attractive.

Nicole and Jordan both waved as their daddy backed out of the parking space. Darren still wasn't speaking to me since the club incident. He didn't even bother to come to the door. He just tooted his horn for Nicole and Jordan to come out, which was cool with me. I didn't have anything to say to him anyway.

Smothered pork chops, black-eyed peas, cornbread and a tossed salad adorned the table set for two. Grover Washington played softly in the background. I took one last look around the apartment and at myself before Mark arrived. I had on a pair of hip-hugger jeans, heels and a nice top. My hair was in a long ponytail, and I wore my favorite perfume, *Temptation*.

Mark arrived right on time. The food was hot; I was brought up in a house where you ate when the food was ready and not a moment later. With the steam still rising from the meal, Mark blessed the table as he held tightly to my hand.

"Looks good."

"And tastes good, too."

"So, you know you can cook, huh?"

"It's edible. I've been cooking since I was twelve years old. Had to. Momma worked late, so I had to fill in until she got home."

Before I finished my sentence, Mark had already devoured one of his pork chops.

"Girl, this is more than edible. You can burn."

"I know. I just wanted you to taste it for yourself."

Momma always said, "The way to a man's heart is first through his stomach." By the satisfied look on Mark's face as he licked his lips and fingers, my journey had already begun. After dinner, Mark helped me clear the dishes as the music continued to play. Mark seemed relaxed and really enjoyed the music—so much so that each time he entered the kitchen with a dish or glass he did the "cha-cha" dance. At one point, he took the rag out of my hand, grabbed me by the waist and spun me around the room. I laughed so loud I thought I would disturb the neighbors.

We moved from the kitchen to the couch. With the lights dimmed more than usual, Mark and I talked softly. His voice was so soothing and seductive. He was the lure and I was definitely the bait. Mark leaned into me and warmly gave a closed-mouth kiss, on my lips, for the first time. It had been a while since I felt so soft, so wanted. Mark moved in closer. My body froze with the rush of excitement. Boy, did I want him. With his hands caressing both sides of my face, his tongue penetrated the crease of my lips. Though his eyes were closed, I could still read them. My mind raced with thoughts. Oh, this feels so good. But is this too soon? Mark moved his hands to my back as he pulled me in closer. I can't believe I am kissing a deacon. But old dude can kiss. His lips are so soft. Mark's touch aroused deep places within me. A few intense minutes passed before I reached the place right before the point of no return. I broke away, lifting myself off the couch. Mark wiped his lips with his thumb, as did I.

"Would you like a piece of cheesecake?"

"I sure would," Mark replied with a grin. However from his tone, he wasn't talking about the same cake I was.

Mark sat at attention (in many ways) as I handed him his dessert, looked at the clock and then back at him. He read my thoughts as he got up and headed for the door.

"Are you sure I have to go? Ain't no telling when we can see each other again," he asked handing the plate back.

"I'll see you on Sunday, as usual."

"That's not what I meant," Mark replied.

"I know," I said as I opened the front door. Mark went to his car without turning around.

When the phone rang, I knew who it was. Nosy-butt Regina.

"So, how did your first date go?" she said without a hello. Regina also went to New Life Baptist and sorta kinda knew who Mark was.

"Fine," I said, still excited from Mark's touch.

"Really?" Regina sounded surprised.

"Yeah, we really didn't do much. You know—I cooked, we ate. We sat and talked and…." I intentionally left Regina hanging.

"And what? Did he try to kiss you?" Regina exclaimed.

"He did more than that. Old boy had his hands all over me."

"The deacon," Regina responded with surprise.

"No, Mark."

## CHAPTER TWO

Lawd, thank Ya, for allowing us to rise anotha morning. While we slept and slumbered, Lawd, You watched over us. We could be dead sleeping in our graves, but Lawd, You saw fit to touch us one mo' time with Ya finga of love. Thank You, Lawd. Father, You're the lily of the valley and the bright and morning star. Lawd, You're a bridge over troubled water. So we say to Ya, Lawd, this morning, Thank Ya, Fatha." The deacon paused before he continued, "Finally, for those who know a word of prayer, please pray my strength in the Lawd, that I may grow stronger and deeper in Him." The deacon rose from his knee and limped back to his seat.

"Shoot," I said, disgusted with myself for being late to church. And not only was I late, but I had to sit in the back of the sanctuary—something I wasn't used to at all. I like the front better. Anyway, it was offering time (yes, I was that late), and as I walked around the altar, I saw Mark on the front pew and waved. He looked right through me as if I wasn't even there. I'm sure he was just preoccupied doing his "deacon thing." As I took my seat, the pastor rose to the podium to give his sermon.

When it came time for the Word of God, most folks seemed

to be in some form of rapture, fixated on every word that came from the preacher as he stood behind the clear Plexiglas pulpit. The preacher preached (in the south we call it hoopin') as if the words that sprung forth from his mouth were the last words anyone would ever hear. His voice was so forceful every time he said the name, Jeeee…sus. And all I know is that when he spoke that name, something on the inside of me jumped to attention. I don't know what Scriptures he based his message on, but he made them all sound so good. And by the looks of everyone else in the congregation, they felt good, too. Oh my word, what an incredible, emotional experience. It was as if something down on the inside of me urged me to stand and to shout. Everything in my hearing on that morning seemed to wreak havoc on my insides. I tried to contain myself, but before my mind could say no to my feet, it was too late. My feet danced to their own rhythmic beat. My hands reached toward the sky as my heart prayed and hoped to touch the One who had allowed me to be. Simultaneously, my mouth opened up and began to say words I hadn't said or thought of before. I danced and praised God for as long as I could.

After service, I tried to make my way to the front so I could at least say hello to Mark before attending the final new members' class. As I did so, I overheard several conversations, but one really stood out.

"Girl, ain't he cute?" the petite woman with a cute face said to her slightly older friend. "And, he's a deacon," she added.

"He don't look old enough to be a deacon," the older woman said.

"Yeah, I know, but he is. He's the youngest on the board."

"Girl, you know I likes my men that way. Hell, the younger the better. From what I see in him, I can sho'll teach him some things he can't find in his *Word*." The woman licked her finger like a piece of fried chicken.

The two women hunched over each other and giggled like schoolgirls.

I interrupted them, "Excuse me, can I get by please?" I didn't know who they were talking about, but I knew I didn't want to hear any more of their conversation. Not waiting for a response, I pushed myself between them. As I approached Mark, I had a big smile on my face. He smiled, too, as I got closer. Man was he handsome. But just as I opened my mouth, he mouthed to me, "Can I call you later?" and then he reached across me to greet the same two women I had just overheard.

I went into the meeting.

"Okay, everybody. Before we get started, does anyone have any questions?" the associate pastor asked. I was the first one in the class to raise my hand. "Yes, Ma'am. What's your question?"

"Yes. Umm. Umm. Can you explain the difference between getting saved and going to church? Or are they both the same?"

The deacon smiled at me as he glanced around the room at the others. They nodded as if they too wanted to ask the same question. He sat down in the steel, padded chair with one leg outstretched and the other with a slight bend.

"No. They're not the same. Going to church is an external, physical act. Lots of people go to church for different reasons. Many go to church for years and still live the same way they did before they ever started going to church. But salvation, what you referred to as 'getting saved,' is an internal, heart issue. True salvation changes the heart. The heart then changes the mind. The mind then changes your actions. And you become a new person, what we refer to as being born again."

31

The associate pastor picked up his Bible and flipped through the pages.

"Young lady, did you bring your Bible?" He directed his question to me.

Nodding my head yes, I reached under my seat and proudly showed it to him. The others followed my lead.

"Let me back up what I'm saying by what God says. Turn in your Bible to the book of Romans, chapter ten, verses nine and ten."

There was a small chorus of pages turning.

The associate pastor began to read, " *'For if you confess with your mouth that Jesus is Lord and believe in your heart that God raised Him from the dead, you will be saved. For it is by believing in your heart that you are made right with God, and it is by confessing with your mouth that you are saved.'*

"As you just read, nowhere in that passage does it tie salvation with church attendance. Now, don't get me wrong, church is important. That's why we are having this meeting. The Bible does state that we should not forsake the assembly of believers. Believers are those of us who believe in Christ. This building, God's house, is where the collective body of believers comes together in agreement and learns from the Word of God. It is a place where we can gather corporately and celebrate the goodness and blessings of God. We get renewed and strengthened here through our worship and praise of God. We come here for a common goal and purpose, to worship, praise and serve God.

"Did I answer your question?" he asked.

We looked like bobble-heads as we all nodded in the affirmative.

"Any more questions?"

I had more questions I wanted to ask, but I didn't. They were *really* personal and I figured I needed a little, okay a lot, of one-on-one time.

~~~~~~~~

Before even placing the car in park, I heard music blaring from Darren's open window. As I got closer to the door, I heard laughter from inside. I rang the doorbell several times, but no one answered. So, I banged on the door. Angrily, an unfamiliar woman opened the door. All I saw was her belly ring attached to what looked like a deep hole. She had to be every bit of six-two, three fifty or so pounds.

"What, heffa," she said as she glared down at me.

"Excuse me?"

"Oh, I'm sorry. I thought you were somebody else." She turned and walked back inside. "Darren, someone's at the door for you," she hollered.

Holding the storm door open, I peeked in. The heavy smoke from inside burned my eyes, so I closed the door and waited. And waited. And waited. Each minute that passed I got hotter and hotter. Finally, I got tired of waiting and walked in. Three gentlemen sitting at the table smoking blunts pointed me to the kitchen. While turning the corner, I saw my baby girl sitting on the lap of some stranger. I ran over and snatched Nicole up like a rag doll. Darren jumped up from his seat and hollered, "What in the hell do you think you're doing?"

Nicole's soft brown eyes looked at me with confusion. I held on tightly to her as I looked around the room for Jordan. Darren saw the direction my eyes were looking and grabbed Jordan before

I could.

"Momma," Jordan said as he reached out his little arms for me.

"It's okay, boy. Yo daddy's gotcha now," Darren said purposely.

The vibration from my cell phone startled me.

"Yeah, you betta get that. It might be ya boy."

The men in the room looked at me, and I stared right back at them.

Darren was talking about Greg, the married man I had slept with while I was still married to him. I ignored the call and took a deep breath. My heart was racing and my pressure had risen to an all time high level. A few beads of sweat began to form on the edges of my brow.

"Darren, can we not do this today, in front of the kids?" I asked as calmly as I could.

"Niqué, you can't control jack up in my house." Darren tightened his grip on Jordan's hand as he tried to come to me. "Boy, be still," he said to Jordan.

"Jordan, Momma is right here. I'm not going anywhere without you, I promise." I smiled at Jordan to reassure him.

"Go on, boy. I'll see you two next week," Darren said as he let go of Jordan's hand and sat back down at the table. He picked up his beer with one hand and his dominoes with the other. "Whose turn is it?" I heard him ask as I grabbed Jordan by the hand and walked out of the house.

"Momma, why is Daddy so mad at you?" Nicole asked as she buckled her own seat belt.

"I don't know, baby," I replied, but in my heart I knew why he was still so upset. I had an affair with a married man. *And,* I had betrayed him in the worst way so that there was no going back.

## CHAPTER THREE

"Moniqué, I'll see you tonight, eight o'clock, my place," Mark announced after he left precise driving directions to his home on my answering machine.

"A picnic?" I said as I walked into Mark's home exactly at eight o'clock. I saw a basket placed on a blanket atop his hardwood floors.

"Yeah, I thought you would enjoy one," Mark said as he held my hand and helped me down onto the blanket.

"Excuse the place. I'm in the process of remodeling the whole house," Mark said as he pointed to the empty room, bare walls and windows.

"What kind of music do you like?" Mark asked as he headed toward the only furniture he had in the room, his entertainment center.

"Now, I listen mostly to gospel and jazz," I said as I noticed that Mark had already placed a CD in the player.

I smiled when I heard the music. He played one of my favorite CDs, *Allen and Allen*, gospel jazz. Mark sat down beside me and placed the basket filled with food between his muscular legs.

"Can I take you to Europe?" Mark asked as he had my usual full attention.

"Excuse me?"

"Can I take you to Europe?" Mark asked again as he opened the basket. Reaching inside, he pulled out bread, cheese, wine, pepperoni, grapes and chicken.

"Okay, you're going to have to explain this," I said looking at all of the items on the blanket.

"Girl, haven't you traveled before?" Mark kidded. "The bread is from Germany; the cheese is from Holland; the wine is from France; the pepperoni is from Italy; the grapes are from Spain, and the chicken, that's from Popeye's," Mark said as his tongue stroked his bottom lip.

"Popeye's isn't in Europe," I said.

"I know, but I had a taste for some chicken, and Popeye's is down the street," Mark said as he made himself a plate. Mark took a grape from the vine, kissed it and placed it in my mouth. Closing my eyes, I ate it, slowly. I savored every drop of juice it produced. "Look, I flew around the world for this food, the least you can do is fix your own plate." He smiled the loveliest smile I had seen in a while as he handed me a plastic plate.

Mark was unusually talkative. Our conversation was easy and our topics varied. One minute we talked politics, the weather, even about the zoo. The next minute, I found myself wrapped in nothing but satin and Mark's muscular arms. The coolness of the sheets contrasted the heat of Mark's thrusts inside me. His hands held my back as I took hold of the bedpost on his California-size sleigh bed. Our mutual pleasure, verbalized only in boisterous moans and groans, was harmony to our ears.

Waking up and getting dressed three hours later, Mark walked me to his door and said as I left, "I had a wonderful night."

"Me, too," I said as he closed the door behind me.

Before I knew it, that one night turned into many nights.

## CHAPTER FOUR

After taking a few sips of water, I glanced up and saw my friend, Linda, heading toward the cafeteria. With water still in my mouth, I was able to get her attention by waving my hands in the air. She nodded in response as she acknowledged my presence.

"Hey, Moniqué," she said.

"Linda," I said as I winced in pain.

"What's wrong with your hands?"

"Child, the nurse said I had carpal tunnel."

Linda took hold of my hands and gently stroked them. She smiled and whispered, "It's done, in Jesus's name." A warm sensation began at my hands, moved up my arms and rested at my elbows. Spiritual victory rang through Linda's vocal chords.

But, that was Linda, a gentle giant. She had a smile and a word of encouragement each time I saw her. From the moment we met five years ago, Linda's trademark had been her smile.

I'll never forget how she and I met for the first time over lunch. I remember sitting down with Linda and another co-worker, Angie. I kinda knew Angie, but I didn't know Linda at all. Our conversation turned to the events of the weekend. I announced proudly, "I'm going to get drunk, like I do every weekend the kids go to their dad's house." Angie laughed and said, "You go girl."

Linda, well, she just looked at me and smiled. Talk about first impressions. Somehow, some way, we became instant friends.

Ever so slowly, our conversations turned toward Christ. At first, I thought Linda was nice to me because I was lost (lost to Christ). But I was so wrong. Linda didn't push her God on me at all. As a matter of fact, if we talked about God at all, it was because I mentioned God first. But boy, when we did talk about God, Linda's eyes filled with joy and her voice rang with excitement. Linda said things like, "Moniqué, God is so good to me that if He didn't do another thing for me, for the rest of my life, He's already done enough." Man, what a statement that was. As I spent time with Linda, she excited me so that I wanted to know the God she knew.

~~~~~~~~~

My church held a Bible conference at a local high school. It was my first real church conference and I was eager to attend. Compared to others, I felt like my growth as a Christian was stagnated for some reason. It just seemed like everybody else had a better understanding and connection with church and God. They were somehow more spiritual, more holy, more *something* more than me. I mean, I went to church. I had a Bible (although I never read it other than Sundays) just like they did and even went to an occasional weekday service here and there. How come I didn't know God like they did?

The first person in the classroom as other church members

strolled in a few minutes later was none other than me. When Mark entered the room, we made immediate eye contact with each other and smiled. Mark looked exceptionally nice, but then again, I knew he would. There was one thing Mark definitely did well, and that was dress. He took great pride in what he wore and it showed.

Mark pulled out a chair for another member of the church and looked around the room for a seat for himself. He found a seat across the room from me and sat down. Immediately, I looked to my right at the empty seat beside me. Mark looked over at me and winked. With his thumb to his ear and his pinky finger at his mouth, he said silently, "I'll call you later." That meant he was doing his deacon thing and "we" had to be on the DL (down low). To my knowledge, no one in church knew that he and I had a sexual relationship at the time.

Without whispering, I answered, "Okay."

After about twenty minutes or so, the instructor came in. "Hello, everyone. Please forgive me for being tardy. But if you want a preacher to show up on time, you've got to have food."

The room erupted in laughter. I could tell by the way the instructor came into the room, he was definitely a people person. With his head lowered, he began to pull stacks of disorganized papers from his expensive, snake-skinned briefcase. As he continued readying himself, he pulled his tie tighter and adjusted his pants to his waist. I surmised he was at ease being the center of attention. He spoke matter-of-factly with a sort of down-home flavor. His choice of words revealed his education, and his mannerisms, like the fact that he put his hands on his hips, told of his country upbringing. He was no more than five-three or five-five, and because of his stocky/overweight build, you could tell the brotha hadn't missed a meal in quite some time. There was something in his overall tone that seemed familiar to me, as if I had seen him somewhere before.

Swiftly, the instructor turned from the blackboard and faced the anticipating class, "My name is Shaun Richardson, associate pastor for Grace Temple."

Naw, it can't be, was my immediate reaction. Surveying the room, Shaun looked at me and, noticeably to everyone in the room, stopped speaking in mid-sentence. I almost died right there on the spot. I quickly turned my head, as I was shy and embarrassed all at the same time. I didn't know how to respond. I mean, what could I do? Should I acknowledge him in a room full of folks, not to mention Mark, or should I play it off like nothing happened?

I chose the latter and then purposefully looked in Mark's direction. Boy, you should have seen the look on Mark's face. I'm not too sure if green is supposed to look like that. Granted, I've seen Mark's impersonation of the Hulk before. Like when we were at the mall and a male acquaintance spoke to me. Or when I was home and the phone rang. Before I could even put the receiver down, he asked, "Who was that?"

This time in the classroom was different. It kinda felt good to see him react that way. You know, the cave man that protected his woman kinda thing. "You go, boy," I cheered inside my head, while I prayed my body language didn't reflect my thoughts.

The instructor apparently recognized me. At least he thought he did, and I him. He quickly regrouped and continued with the lesson. After the class, I went over to speak to him. I wanted to shake his hand and tell him how much I really enjoyed the class.

I started to open my mouth when he said, "Moniqué Clark."

Right away I knew I had gone to high school with him because only people from high school knew me by my maiden name Clark. He grabbed me and hugged me tightly. It was one of those snug, granddad hugs. After I caught my breath, I finally recognized his face and put it with his name.

"Shaun. It's so nice to see you," I said as the women behind me began to push a little.

I stepped to the side, allowing them to get to Shaun before they exploded.

Shaun mouthed to me, "Can you stay for a minute?"

I nodded yes.

Once the line of well-wishers disappeared, Shaun and I resumed talking. We embraced once again (now that I knew who it was I was hugging) and soon caught up on what had been happening in our respective lives. I only told him the good parts.

Everyone from the class had left, even Mark. For a brief second, I wondered when Mark had walked out. I thought it was awfully rude of him not to say anything to me before he left. A part of me was tired of the DL, especially then. But again, that was par for the course with Mark. No public attention, just private affection. Maybe he said good-bye and I just didn't hear him. Anyway. It was late and Shaun and I had to exit the building.

"Where did you park?" Shaun questioned.

"Right around the corner."

"I'll walk you out."

Shaun and I talked the entire time. It seemed like we tried to squeeze the last several years of our lives into the hundred or so yards we had to walk to our cars.

"Well, you know I'm a minister," he said as he stated the obvious.

"Yeah, and by the looks of things, a good one, too." Laughing,

45

I looked at his mid-section.

"So, how long have you been saved, Moniqué?"

"Good question, Shaun. I really don't know how to answer you." I paused. "At twelve, I remember accepting Jesus Christ into my heart at a youth revival in Momma's old church, New Hope. And, about nine months ago, I started going back to church, rededicated my life to Christ and now, here I am."

Shaun laughed as I finished my statement.

"All I know is that I don't remember when it happened, the exact time or day of the week. I just know it *did* happen."

Shaun said, "Sounds good to me."

The parking lot, filled with cars a few short hours earlier, had almost cleared out. Immersed in our conversation, my peripheral vision caught a glimpse of Mark as he rode by. Mark rolled down his window and yelled, "Moniqué Kennedy. Get in your car and go home!"

I was dumbfounded. On Mark's face was a smile (well, let's just call it one) that told of his jealousy and insecurity. For the second time in one evening, I was embarrassed beyond words. Shaun raised one of his eyebrows and looked at me. I couldn't say or do anything, so I played it off.

Jokingly, I pushed Shaun's shoulder and said, "Men—can't live with 'em, can't live without 'em. Hey, are you free to go to dinner?"

"Now?" Shaun asked.

"Yeah, if that's okay?"

Shaun followed me to the nearest Denny's, and we found a secluded area in the back and sat.

"So, do I call you Shaun or do I have to call you 'Reverend'?" I asked.

"Girl, call me anything but the n—word." He chuckled aloud, which revealed his bulging stomach. "Look, Moniqué. I'm just like everyone else, really I am." He spoke looking above the rim of his glasses. "Call me Shaun, please."

"Cool," I said, as I sighed in relief. From that moment on, I felt at ease with him, and if I said so myself, he felt at ease with me. Shaun was an excellent listener and just a good, down-to-earth person. He seemed genuinely concerned about my welfare, especially when it came to men, or should I say, Mark.

"So, tell me about that clown in the parking lot," Shaun said as he called me out.

"Mark?" I said. I knew full well whom he meant. "Well, what do you want to know?"

"Tell me something about him," Shaun said as he pretended to read the menu.

My cell vibrated against my waist. "Can you hold that thought a minute? I need to get this."

"Sure," Shaun said as he read the menu for real that time.

"Hello?"

"You have two messages waiting. Would you like to hear them now?"

I had forgotten that I had my messages forwarded to my cell. Pressing the appropriate key, the first message played. It was a hang up, again. There had been several of them in the last few weeks. The final message automatically played, "Call me, when you get a free minute. It's important."

Shaun read the troubled look on my face, "Is everything okay?"

"Yeah," I said as Shaun began to talk. But I wasn't really listening. The last message stunned me a bit, and I didn't know what to do about it. I shrugged my shoulders as I heard Shaun say, "So, do you have any questions you want to ask me?"

Boy did I. I bombarded him. "Why is Scripture so hard to understand? What does it mean to study the Word? Why can't I seem to remember and recite Scripture that I have read? Why does God seem to talk to everyone else but me? Why do I keep sinning when I try not to? Why does God…?"

Shaun interrupted me.

"Whoa. Take a deep breath and wait a minute," he said as he grinned from ear to ear. "I see right now we have a long way to go. But you're on the right track. You have a real zeal and zest for knowledge. God will use that in you."

"But what does all that mean, Shaun?" I said, frustrated.

"It means this," he paused as he chose his words carefully, "Moniqué, take your time. Your walk with God is like no one else's. God will deal with you on an individual basis. Don't compare your growth or knowledge of Him to anyone. *And*, spiritual growth does not happen overnight. It's a process we all must go through. When you get home, read this Scripture, 2 Corinthians 5:17. Paraphrasing, it says, *When a man or woman is in Christ, he is a new creature, person; old things, the things you used to do, you no longer do, and behold, all things are becoming new*." Shaun went on to say, "Now, pay close attention to the word 'becoming'. It means a process. It's ongoing and never-ending. Each day in Christ you will change and become new because as people, we change," Shaun said as he peered over the framed edge of his glasses.

"Oh." That's all I managed to say out of my mouth. Suddenly, a giant light bulb went off in my head. Shaun made the Scripture so easy to understand.

Shaun added one more thing.

"You're new to the church, and there are many wolves waiting to get a bite out of you. Pray and ask God for His direction and His protection as you go through this process."

Although I sat at the table with Shaun, my mind and thoughts had already raced to Mark.

~~~~~~~~

Closing the door behind me, I sat on the couch and picked up the phone and dialed Mark's number.

Click...

"Hello. Sorry, but I'm not home at the moment, but if you'd like, leave a message at the tone and I will return your call. Have a blessed day," his machine said.

"Great, his answering machine." Without hesitation, I looked for the time. The clock read eleven forty-five. I thought, Where is he. He should be home by now.

After the beep, I said, "Yeah, Mark, it's me. I'd like to talk to you about this evening. Give me a call when you get in. By the way, this is Moniqué." For some strange reason, I felt it necessary to mention my name.

1:25 a.m. and no return phone call from Mark. I got into bed.

3:47 a.m. and Mark's phone rang ten times without an answer.

5:15 a.m. I fell asleep with the phone still in my hand.

## CHAPTER FIVE

Walking hand-in-hand with Nicole and Jordan, we made our way into Chuck E. Cheese on a Saturday afternoon. Kids were everywhere as Nicole and Jordan jumped in excitement.

"C'mon, Momma, we're missing it."

"Boy, you better be still and stop that jumping," I said as the teenager who tried to put the thingy around Jordan's wrist became a bit frustrated. Poking Jordan's head with my finger, I gave him a look only a momma could give. But I quickly smiled because I wanted the day to be special for all of us. Seemed like moments like these were so few and far between with the job, their homework, grocery shopping, laundry and housecleaning; that all had to be done. Let alone trying to date someone. Finally getting the opportunity to spend quality time with the kids was just a blessing.

Jordan and Nicole bolted for the play area as I looked around for a table and for Mark. He mentioned earlier on the phone that he might stop by.

"Hey there."

"Hey, yourself." I was surprised to see Shaun at Chuck E.

Cheese of all places. "What are you doing here?"

"What, a man can't come to Chuck E. Cheese on a Saturday with a room full of screaming, whining, crying children?"

"I didn't say that, but...."

"Girl, ease up. I'm just trippin'. See those two little girls over there." He pointed to a set of twins dressed in red and white.

"Aw, they're so cute," my voice whined.

"Yeah, they get their good looks from their uncle. I'm doing the uncle thing today."

"That's nice," I said as I looked over Shaun's shoulder checking on Nicole and Jordan. I was paranoid about the child abduction/molestation epidemic in the country. I wasn't going to let nobody, and I mean nobody, take or hurt my babies.

"So what's been up, young lady, since we last spoke?"

"Not much."

"You still going to church?"

"Yeah."

"Are you seeing anybody?" Shaun asked all out of the blue.

My eyes went straight to his ring finger.

"No, not really," I lied. I'm not sure why.

"Are you sure? You don't sound too convincing."

"I've had a few dates with a friend, here and there."

"Does he go to your church?" Shaun tried to ask without prying too much.

"Yes. He's actually a deacon there."

"A deacon?"

I looked again, but this time over Shaun's other shoulder.

Shaun turned around.

"Is that him over there?" Shaun inquired.

"No, but you have seen him before."

52

"Where?"

"Do you remember the guy that was in the parking lot?"

"Oh dude." Shaun's face frowned.

In the background, I heard Jordan scream, "Mommy, Mommy, Mommy. Hurry." I immediately turned both my attention, time and body direction away from Shaun. I had to find out what was happening to the most important man in my life. As I made my way to Jordan, I gave a quick, "Excuse me. I'll talk to you later."

Later never came. After Shaun and his nieces left, me and the kids did, too. Mark never did show up, well, at Chuck E. Cheese, that is.

~~~~~~~~~

"I thought you were coming by this morning."

"I know, baby, but I got tied up with a few meetings, but hey, I'm here now," Mark said petting my hand on the table.

"That you are," I said, reading the Steakhouse menu without looking up at him.

"I'm hungry. What about you?" Mark rubbed his flat stomach and poked out his lips.

I loved his lips. I broke out in a wide smile, lusting over him.

"Mo, I think it's time we take this relationship to the next level. What do you think?"

My insides shook. *Marriage.*

"What level would that be?" My eyes were wide as excitement bubbled within.

"Well, you already have my heart."

"I do?"

"Girl, stop trippin'. You know I love you."

Although I loved Mark dearly, he hadn't actually come out and said the words before—whereas I had said them numerous times to him.

"You do?" I said as the waiter came to take our order.

"Let's talk about this later, okay? I can come over tonight, right?"

The bubbles subsided. It must have been gas.

After making love and before we fell asleep, I reminded Mark he had to leave first thing in the morning. Stephanie was bringing the kids home before noon. By now, Mark knew the routine. The next morning I arose early. Glancing over at the clock, it was 6:34 a.m. I thought, "Lord, just a few more minutes please." Mark rolled over as I noticed the peaceful look on his face. I rubbed his cheek softly trying not to wake him yet. There was a faint knock at the door.

I looked at the clock again. Six thirty-seven in the morning. Stephanie was early! And she had the kids with her. But she would use her key, I thought as I walked to the front door, grabbing the ties to my robe.

I peeked out of the peephole. It had begun to rain. I didn't see anyone, but just as I turned to walk away, there it was again.

Tap, tap, tap.

"Who is it?" There was no answer. So I asked again, only this time I got louder. "Who is it?" Perched on my tiptoes, I scarcely saw the top of the person's head. Whoever it was had their head down to avoid the fine mist of rain steadily coming down.

I heard a small voice that said, "Toni."

"Excuse me?" I didn't know a Toni.

Speaking up, the woman said, "Is Mark there?"

She had to have known he was there, because his car was parked right outside. On the other hand, she might have had to knock on several other apartment doors to find out which apartment he was in. Or, the heffa (oops, that's my momma coming out of me) just got lucky on the first knock. Anyhow, there was still a woman on my doorstep asking for my man. My heart sank, but my blood pressure rose as I started to get that sick, queasy, nervous type of feeling. Having felt it before, I knew it wasn't good. I said to the voice on the other side of my door, "Excuse me?"

She said louder and forcibly, "Mark Hayes. Is he there?"

I opened the door, wide.

For a brief moment, I tried to make sense of it all. Mark was a deacon in the church. Deacons counsel men *and* women all the time. So the person on the other side of the door must be a parishioner who needed Deacon Hayes's assistance or counseling, right? But Mark *always* kept his private life…private.

I don't know how, but I kept my cool.

"Come in, but wait right here," I said as I pointed to a spot on the wall by the door. I went to the bedroom. No, let me correct myself. I went to MY bedroom and awakened my partner of eleven months and twenty-nine days (one day short of one year. You know how we women can keep track of days).

"Wake up," I said as I tapped Mark softly on his bare shoulder.

"Huh," he grumbled, his eyes closed.

"Wake up. You have a visitor in the living room waiting for you." That really got his attention. Mark's eyes revealed his nervousness.

"Who is it?" he asked me.

I thought to myself, "Boy, you betta get your behind up and

see for yourself."

Mark must have read the expression on my face because two seconds later he was half-dressed and had walked out of the bedroom. And me, I was right behind him. My hands were sweating.

"What are you doing here?" were Mark's first words to her.

"I'm looking for you. What are YOU doing here?" she retorted.

For three to five minutes, Mark and Toni went back and forth as to why he was with me and vice versa. I finally got fed up. "Look, Toni, this is *my* house and I want you to leave. Apparently you know Mark, so I will suggest that you see him at his house." I glared at Mark and said, "Please escort your friend to her car."

As Mark reached for Toni's left arm, she got up in my face. "Honey, I don't know what Mark has told you, but I am with him. As a matter of fact, I know his behind better than the back of my own hand."

I felt my old self rising within me. I really didn't want to have to come out of my robe. So, I opened the door and pointed for both of them to get out. It was obvious to me that Toni wasn't your normal, every day, run-of-the-mill church parishioner.

While Mark and Toni were outside in the rain, I tried desperately to peek out of the peephole to see what was going on. I only heard maybe two words out of every ten said, but I tried to listen anyway. After about seven minutes or so crept by, I couldn't take it any longer.

I swung the door open and insisted, "Mark, get yo butt in here," directing my daring gaze at Toni, taunting her.

Mark was frozen in his tracks, so I sternly repeated myself, although I was certain my words needed no repetition. "Mark, now."

"Mark, you be'd not move a muscle," Toni told *my man* and evidently *her man* as well. At that point, I knew God was with me and not my enemies. Because to my own surprise and amazement, I did not curse her out nor did I kick her tiny butt at that moment. Without a word spoken out of my mouth, I looked in Mark's direction. He came when I looked at him. I closed the door behind him for some much-needed privacy.

"I don't know exactly what's going on here, but I do know it ain't right." I knew deep down inside what was going on, but my heart couldn't take it. "Please ask her to leave my home," I said again.

Toni was peeking through the window.

Mark did as I asked and came right back in. I paced the floor for about half an hour. Mark followed my every footstep.

"Moniqué, you have to believe me. Me and that girl are just friends. I don't know why she is trippin' like this," he said as he tried to convince me his words were true.

"Mark, I was born on *a day*, not yesterday. No woman in her right mind is gonna get up out of her bed looking for some man at six something in the morning just because they're friends."

"But I swear we're just friends. We used to date...." I cut him a look that went straight through him.

Mark stuttered, "Uh, uh, uh. But we stopped long before you and I met," he insisted.

I couldn't believe my eyes or my ears. Mark was practically on his knees as he pleaded with me.

"Baby girl. I love you and only you."

I tuned him out. His words were too painful to hear.

The betrayal hit me to the core. It was like nothing I had ever felt in my life.

Mark was saved. He was in the church. *He was supposed* to be different, set apart. I wasn't sure who betrayed me more, Mark or God.

My heart crumbled at that exact moment.

"You gotta go. Now," I demanded.

Mark didn't press the issue as he headed toward the room; he had to finish dressing. After returning from the bedroom, Mark bent down to kiss me, but I turned my head.

The door closed quietly behind him as the floodgates of memories gushed through my thoughts. So that was who he had late night meetings with. Sometimes, his butt didn't get home until midnight. Oh, and his excuse for not answering his phone, 'I was beat, so I turned my ringer off.' Why couldn't he just be honest and tell me the truth? It all makes sense to me. Our late night phone calls interrupted—Mark said they were phone solicitors—at two a.m.? Right.

Paranoia began to set in; I couldn't sit still. I betcha that heffa is over his house right now, waiting on him, I thought. It was Sunday morning, Mark had to go home and get ready for church.

I jumped up as fast as I could and got dressed. I drove to Mark's house just as sure as my name was Moniqué.

I pulled in around the corner from his house. I sat at just the right angle where I could see his front door and where he couldn't see me. Mark parked his car in his usual place, across the street from his house. I always wondered why he didn't park his car in his driveway like most normal people did. But that moment wasn't the time to try and figure Mark out. My heart jumped when a car passed by. "Was that her?" I thought each time. Emotionally spent,

I waited outside his home until 9:45, and then I went home. I threw my keys on the table and checked my messages. The light blinked rapidly. All five or so messages were basically the same:

"Moniqué, it's me. Pick up, please."..."I really need to talk to you."..."Come on, Moniqué, please."..."Please, I'll do anything, Moniqué."..."Okay, I gotta go, service is about to begin, I'm gonna call you when I get out, okay?" Mark begged.

It wasn't even eleven o'clock in the morning yet. I skipped church that Sunday.

~~~~~~~~~

I had missed the last three Sundays in a row and decided to attend a mid-week Bible study instead. "Good Evening," I said to the women sitting in front of me as I sat behind them on the pew.

"Good evening," they responded curtly.

I sat in my seat readying myself, when I heard the two women begin their conversation.

"Girl, did you hear about Deacon Hayes?" the slightly older woman spoke first.

"What?" the petite woman with the cute face asked.

The older woman looked to her left and then to her right. "Honey, I heard he was at it again."

"Naw," the cute-faced lady responded.

"Child, they say he done got himself a wife and two women on the side. One's his play thing."

The petite woman with the cute face finished her friend's sentence, "The other one must be his toy."

"But he got caught," the older woman said.

My heart pounded through my blouse as I dropped my Bible on the floor.

"I heard his wife left him," the petite woman said.

"So," the older lady grumbled.

"Actually, I heard she took everything,"

"So," she grumbled more and smacked her lips.

"Child, she even took the stuff off the walls."

My mind flashed back to the first time I was at Mark's home. He told me he was redecorating. Redecorating my a…and Married. He's married! I was going to be sick. I placed my hand over my mouth and just as I did, the two women turned around and looked me square in the eyes. I swear they didn't blink an eyelash. I froze.

"Yeah, it's amazing what you know about folk," the slightly older woman said.

"And you know, the Bible sho'll declares, Galatians six seven, 'In due season, you shall reap what you sow,' " the petite woman with the cute face said.

Embarrassed and ashamed beyond words, I grabbed my purse and Bible and bolted for the door. How in the world was I ever going to walk back in that church again? How did they know?

Who else knew? And for how long? Oh, my God.

Running down the sidewalk towards my car, I had already made up my mind. I wasn't ever going back to that church again. Out of breath, I sat in my seat and cried. "Not again, not again, what is wrong with me? God, please tell me. I can't do this again!" My thoughts drifted back three years and to Greg Hendricks.

I met Greg at a small café outside of town. He was a Senior Major in the Air Force, due to retire, married with children, and having a mid-life crisis. And me, I was just lonely. No other way to put it. Greg told me right from jump street that he was married, which at the time was fine with me; so was I. And the two of us together were perfect.

Greg had a way of looking at me that scared and excited me to the core. He read my every thought and fulfilled my every fantasy. He made me feel soft, warm and feminine. Every moment we spent was a stolen, pleasurable moment. Each time we met, the thrill became addictive, and the associated danger was welcomed with anticipation. I enjoyed calling his house as he talked to me right in front of his wife. He, too, enjoyed riding past my house as Darren and I stood outside in our front yard, playing with the kids. Greg even had the audacity to wave at times. But the fun soon ended for me when my period was late. Scared wasn't even the word for what I was feeling. I didn't immediately know whose baby it was. I had to check my calendar and remember secret dates. But I knew whose baby it wasn't going to be, and that was mine. I hadn't talked to Greg since. But it hadn't stopped him from calling.

~~~~~~~~~

Mark was relentless as he called me at home and at work. It seemed like he called me every hour on the hour. Mad as all get out, I just told him, "Stop calling me. I ain't got nothing to say. And when I do, believe you me, you'll be the first one to know." Mark didn't know that I knew he was married.

As each day passed, I was surprised at the coldness in my heart toward Mark and even more surprised at the ease to which I reverted to my previous ways of thinking concerning relationships and how to respond to traumatic situations. My attitude in the past would have been "to hell with the person and the relationship," and just like then, it was now, to hell with Mark. The jury was still out on where I stood with God.

~~~~~~~~

"He's supposed to be different, set apart, consecrated and holy," I said while walking at a feverish pace on the treadmill. Sweat covered my body.

"Who is?" Linda asked as she placed her feet on the pedals of the Stairmaster right beside me.

"Mark. That's who." I didn't mean to speak to Lin so harshly. "I just don't understand. I went back to church for a change, but instead all I got was what I normally get all the time. Stupid stuff."

"Like what, Mo? What are you trying to say?"

"Lin, Mark's married. And not only that, but the sucker had the audacity to cheat on me with another church member, and it wasn't even his wife!" I pushed the intensity level on the machine up a notch.

"Have you had sex with him?" she asked without looking at me.

I didn't respond. But with Lin, I didn't have to.

"Oh, I see," Linda said looking straight ahead out of the window.

I hit the stop button on the treadmill, sat down on the edge of the machine and put my hands over my face.

"Lin, he's just like you, a deacon!" I lowered my voice as the other employees in the company's fitness center looked over at me.

"Just because he's a deacon and holds a position of authority in the church doesn't mean he hasn't or doesn't sin. He is human just like everyone else. Are you saying that he is somehow different than the average believer? Is that what you're trying to say?" Lin said as she continued her workout.

"Yeah," I said sort of underneath my breath.

"Oh, I thought you were talking about yourself."

"Huh?" I turned around and looked at her. She hadn't even begun to sweat.

"Mo, when you accepted Christ into your life, you became born again?"

"Right."

"Old things were passed away."

"Right."

"And behold a new thing was created, right?"

"Right."

"So, *you* are to be different, set apart, consecrated and holy. Right?"

"Right," I said reluctantly. I felt like a kid who just got caught stealing candy. Her words hit me harder than a brick.

"Mo, you can't put new wine in an old wineskin. Nor can you do what you used to do or think like you used to think and expect a different outcome. You have got to be willing to make some hard, difficult decisions based on where you want to go and be in Christ." Linda never broke her stride on the Stairmaster. "So, who are you really mad at? Mark, for not being who you expected him to be, or are you mad at yourself for not being who you know God has called you to be? For He has called you, Mo, to be set apart, consecrated and holy, not just Mark." Linda looked back at me for the first time.

I turned my head. I suddenly realized Linda's words were

the same as Shaun's. Apparently, I didn't heed to his warning about wolves.

~~~~~~~~

Daydreaming on the drive home from work, I turned the corner into my apartment complex and realized I had forgotten to pick up Nicole and Jordan from the daycare. "Lord, Moniqué, what are you thinking?" I decided to go home first, change my clothes and then pick them up. I still had about thirty minutes before the daycare closed and it was just five minutes away. I hadn't even made it back to my bedroom before I heard a knock on the door.

"Moniqué, open up. It's me, Mark," he shouted.

My mouth hung open as I opened the door. "Oh, so you just gonna come by here anytime you want now. You couldn't call first?" I said with my hand in his face.

"Moniqué, I had to see you. I tried calling you at work today, but you won't talk to me."

"What do you want me to say, boy? 'Why'd you cheat on me?' " I hollered as I stood in the doorway.

"Moniqué, I didn't cheat on you with that girl. How many times do I have to say that?"

"Naw, the point is not how many times. The point is there shouldn't have been any time." I began to close the door.

Mark placed his foot in the door to prevent it from shutting. "Please, Moniqué, let me in," Mark checked his surroundings. "Your neighbors are looking."

"Like I care. They're nosy anyway," I screamed. But I did care. It was bad enough that everyone in the church knew my business; I didn't want my neighbors to know, too. So, I reluctantly let him in.

I stood in the middle of the living room with my arms folded across my chest while Mark walked past me and sat on the couch.

"I didn't say you could sit down. You won't be staying long. Ain't no need for you to get comfortable."

Mark stood up and walked toward me. I plopped down on the other couch, arms still folded across my chest.

"Okay. You got five minutes. I suggest you make them good." I spoke fast.

"Moniqué, what can I say that I haven't already said?"

Flabbergasted, I leaped to my feet and said, "You are kidding, right? I refuse to believe you think I'm that stupid."

"Moniqué, I would never call you stupid," Mark said as he tried to calm me down by speaking in a soft tone.

"Oh, I know you won't call me stupid to my face. You ain't that crazy. However, your actions speak a lot louder than your words. How about you start with your wife's name."

Mark lost two shades to his complexion. "Mo, I'm separated and the divorce will be final in a few weeks from now. I swear, I was going to tell you then."

I didn't believe a word he said. Looking at my watch, "Oh, your time is up. See ya. Don't let the doorknob hit ya where the good Lord split'cha," I said making myself laugh for a brief moment. My intent was to dismiss him like he had dismissed me.

There was a knock on the door.

Frustrated, I didn't even bother to look in the peephole, I just opened it.

Toni. She stood with her hands on her hips, popping a piece of gum. Lord, I lost whatever scruples I had left.

"What in the h...." Before I finished my sentence, Mark pushed me aside and was out the door. He grabbed Toni by both of her arms and slammed her down on her back, right on the top of my car. Boom.

I stood in the doorway watching the struggle in slow motion, unable to move. What I saw reminded me of a bad episode of Jerry Springer. Stuff like that ain't *never* happened to me before I got saved. That kind of thing doesn't happen to saved folks, does it? With all of my might, I tugged and pleaded with Mark to let Toni go. By the look on Toni's face, she was terrified and so was I. Never, and I mean never, had I seen Mark that angry.

Finally, *something* came over him and he released his grip and stepped away. (I think Mark saw himself in prison orange and decided it wasn't his color.) Toni laid there on the car; visibly shaken up.

"My God, why are you here again?" I pleaded. I stood over her as I shook my fists violently at her. "Why can't you leave us alone? If you need to talk to Mark that bad, then why don't you go over to his house?"

Toni stared into the blue sky that overlooked my head.

"Look, Toni, I have two small children, and thank God they're still at the daycare center. If you don't stay away from me and my house, if I have to, I'll call the cops on you."

Mark stood silent on the steps near my door, then hollered out, "Go home, girl. Nobody *here* wants you."

Lord, why did he have to say that? Toni unexpectedly lunged up toward Mark with a vengeance. Clearly, Toni was a woman scorned. But she made one mistake on her way. She pushed me down in the process. She didn't have to go there. But she did. The next thing I knew, I was all over that child. Bandaged hands and all, I punched, pulled, screamed and even yanked out sections of her fake Beyonce-looking weave. What a sight. After a few minutes, Mark pulled the two of us apart. It must have been a fantasy of his to see a cat fight. The skinny child didn't stand a chance against all my hips. She was about my same height but only weighed a hundred pounds soaking wet. And her weave, let it be known, she needed her money back. As she got herself halfway together, she realized that I had pulled off her shirt. Toni ran sobbing toward her car. Jumped in and sped off.

Immediate conviction set in. Oh, I felt so *baaad*. Words couldn't express how truly remorseful I felt. I had lowered my standards. I didn't fight over a man, any man. Momma always said, "Ain't no man worth possibly getting your butt whipped for." I actually didn't fight for Mark. I hit Toni because she pushed me, and I just lost it. Momma also said, "Can't nothing come out of you that ain't already in you." And the Lord knew, I had a lot in me. I thought I had that aspect of my personality under control. Evidently not.

I stormed into the house. Mark tried to put his hands around me, I guess he was trying to console me or something, but I wasn't having it.

"Get yo nasty hands off me. This is all your fault," I snapped. I ran back into my bedroom, locked the door and fell on my knees. I had to talk to God, right then and there. *"Dear God, please, Lord, forgive me for what just happened. Lord, I was so wrong to hit that girl. Please, God, give her traveling mercies driving home. Please, Lord, dry her tears and give her comfort like only You can. Please, oh God, allow me to make this right. Allow me to rise above my circumstances and to correct this situation. God, I pray that You will forgive me of each and every one of my sins and throw them as far as the east is from the west. Please, oh God, help me. I can't do this alone. I need You so much. Please, oh Lord."* I heard a knock on the bedroom door so I ended my prayer. *"This is my prayer, in Jesus's name, Amen."* I wiped the tears from my face, stood and walked over to the locked door. "What," I sighed, then continued, "What do you want?" I yelled at Mark.

"We need to talk."

"Yes, we do need to talk, but not before you call Toni and apologize," I said unlocking and opening the door.

"What? Apologize for what?"

"You heard me. We are going to get this mess straightened out right now. If you can't call or don't wanna call, then give me the number, I will."

"Huh. I ain't calling that bit…," Mark caught his word. "Toni. I'm not calling Toni," he said deliberately.

"Then give me her number. How far does she live from here?"

"Twenty minutes," he said with an attitude.

"Great, she should be home right about now." I handed Mark a piece of paper to write down Toni's number. "Now get out," I said with force just as he wrote the last digit.

"What?" A response Mark had not expected.

"You heard me. Haven't I been ugly enough for one day? Please go. I don't even have the mental energy or strength to fight with you, too, " I said while placing my hands on my forehead.

Mark left quietly. Well, he did mumble something underneath his breath. It sounded a little like, "And I'll be damned."

Waiting a few minutes longer and saying a quick prayer, I called Toni. Speaking to her was a must. I wanted to know if she was okay.

"Hello?"

"Hi, may I speak to Toni?"

"Who's calling?" a protective, but familiar voice demanded.

"My name is Moniqué. Moniqué Clark. Greg?" I asked, confused all of a sudden. My voice quivered.

The protective voice muffled the receiver and began to talk to someone there. The voice, deeper in tone than before, answered me and said, "She's not home." The phone was then snatched away. At first, I heard a whimper. I guessed it was Toni and that she was still quite shaken and upset.

"Hello," she said.

"Toni, this is Moniqué. You just left my house."

"I know your name," she said as her statement surprised me. "I found your name and number in Mark's wallet."

Her relationship with Mark revealed more each time she spoke.

"Well, I called because I was concerned about you. I needed to know that you made it home safely, and I'm so sorry about tonight and my behavior. Is there anything I can do for you?"

"Yeah, you can tell me how long you've been screwing Mark," she asked with a definite sister-girl at-ti-tude.

"We've been dating about a year now," I replied as if I was the one that got caught with her man.

"A year," she screamed.

"So how did you find my house?" a question I really wanted the answer to.

"The Internet," she replied.

After we got over the initial shock of both of our actions, we talked for about a half hour or so. Toni and Mark were once lovers, but that part of their relationship faded out once I got into the picture. (It was nice to know Mark only slept with one of us at a time.) Toni said that she and Mark continued, however, to communicate. Toni had hoped that she and Mark would eventually get back together as a couple one day. She said she was just biding her time. Toni said she got suspicious of Mark when he began reducing the amount of time they spent together. She said he always had an excuse for something. I told her the same thing. We were definitely talking about the same person. Toni expressed how much she loved and adored Mark. As did I. Toni loved him so much that she gave up her virginity to him at eighteen, which prompted my next question.

"How old are you, if you don't mind me asking?"

"I'm nineteen."

My heart sank when she stated her age.

"Are you saved?"

"Yes. I accepted Christ at the altar about two years ago, around March. That's how I met Mark. He came into my new members' meeting and introduced himself to me."

"Excuse me? What did you just say?"

"I met Deacon Hayes, well, Mark, at church," she answered. "How did you two meet?"

"Baby girl, that ain't even relevant right now," I answered. Boy was I pissed. Switching gears for a moment, "Whose number did I dial? Is this your personal home number?" I was now more curious about the man who answered the phone.

"I live with my parents, but you dialed my personal line."

"Who was that who answered the phone?"

"That was my daddy," Toni answered.

"I'm so sorry for all these questions, but may I please ask

just one more?"

"Okay."

"What is your daddy's name?" I asked already knowing the answer in my gut.

"Greg Hendricks," she replied.

My mouth hung wide open.

"Hello? Moniqué? Are you there?"

Stuttering at first, but then my speech becoming clearer, I answered Toni, "Thank you for talking to me and I'm glad you're okay. Please accept my sincere apology, and I wish you the best in the future."

"Thank you for calling," she said, sounding like a little baby. "And, oh, by the way, you won't have anymore hang-ups on your phone or anymore visits by me."

"Thank you," I said as I hung up the phone.

I sighed as I pictured in my mind a little girl hanging up on me. I realized I still had to pick up Nicole and Jordan at the daycare. Panicked because of the time, I got in my car and headed toward the center. I didn't have time to think about the fact that I had just beaten up Mark's ex-lover, Greg's daughter. Rounding the corner like a driver in the Indy 500, the main lights in the daycare center were turned off. I panicked as I walked up to the locked front door and knocked on the black glass window as hard as I could. Mrs. Teresa wobbled up to the glass and gave a half smile. When she opened the door, I began to apologize for my tardiness.

"Mrs. Teresa, I am so sorry. I had a bit of drama at the house and...."

"And your butt is too trifling to come and get your kids on time." Darren's big head revealed itself behind Mrs. Teresa's wide back as he spoke angrily. "I'm home minding my own business and I get a damn phone call from here. Where were you? And why couldn't you come and get my kids?"

"Why are you here?" I asked Darren and then posed the same question to Mrs. Teresa.

"Well, since you were not here at closing, we had to notify your emergency contact."

"I am so sorry about the confusion, but let's get one thing straight right now. He is not to be contacted at all."

"Mrs. Kennedy, you did not have that stated on your emergency contact sheet."

I thought back and remembered that I had forgotten to change the form after our divorce was finalized almost a year-and-a-half ago.

"My bad. Well, I'm here now, Darren, you can go. I got them."

"Always trying to handle me. Woman, when you gonna realize you can't touch this," Darren smiled and rested his strong, black hand on his crotch. He then squeezed the front of his pants like a fresh lemon. "My babies are coming with me. I'ma take them to my momma's for a few. I'll drop them off in an hour. Cool?"

I didn't want to cause another scene, so I shook my head yes and began to walk away.

Jordan called out my name.

"Momma, what's that?" asked Jordan as he pointed his small finger to the bandages wrapped around both of my wrists. Jordan spoke quickly before Nicole had a chance to dominate his time with me.

"It's something to help Momma's hands," I softly replied.

"What's wrong, Momma?" He was frustrated by my lack of a satisfactory response.

"Jordan," Nicole snapped, "stop asking Momma so many questions. You know what we are supposed to ask her first," her wise ten-year-old self said without pausing once for a breath of air.

"Oh yeah, Ma...how was your day?" Jordan quickly asked.

I laughed through the pain in my wrists as well as the pain in my heart.

Darren called out to the kids, "C'mon now, we gotta go." Nicole and Jordan always had a way of turning my bad days into something magical and beautiful. And that daughter of mine, Nicole, never missed a detail. When Nicole was five years old, on her first day of kindergarten, I gave her two brand new quarters. Handing her the first quarter, I said, "Nicole, this quarter is for your breakfast."

"Okay, Momma," she said like a big girl.

"Now, Nicole, this quarter is for your lunch. Okay?" I handed her the last quarter that was in my hand.

"I understand, Momma."

I knelt down and gave her a kiss on the lips. She had such small pink lips. I knew I must have kissed Nicole at least twenty times a day. While watching her as she sat in her seat, a small tear fell from my eyes as the yellow bus drove away. My baby girl was growing up. Later that afternoon, as I picked Nicole up from after-school care, she walked with her head down to the car. Not expecting that reaction from my daughter on her first day of kindergarten, I was alarmed. I ran and met her halfway, squatted down to her eye level and asked her, "Nicole, baby, what's wrong?" I wanted to know because whatever it was, it was going to be fixed.

"Momma, I'm so hungry," she whimpered.

"Why are you hungry? Did you lose the money Momma gave you?" I wondered if some mean old bully had stolen her money or something. With her two small hands, Nicole reached into her pocket and pulled out the two quarters I had given her earlier and handed them to me.

"Nicole, why didn't you use the quarters Momma gave you?" I was confused.

"Because Momma, I couldn't remember which quarter was for breakfast and which quarter was for lunch," she said emphatically.

"Lord," I thought to myself, "have I created a monster." I felt so guilty for stressing, and apparently overstressing, to my children the value of listening and obeying my every word. I drove immediately to the nearest McDonalds. I told my baby, "Order any and everything you want from the menu," and she did exactly that.

## CHAPTER SIX

As I carried my tray into the cafeteria, I spotted Linda by the window sitting by herself. "Lin, let me tell you about my dream last night," I said placing my tray down on her table.

"Hold on, let me put some hot sauce on this first."

"Ooo wee, that's a lot," I said wrinkling up my face at her French fries.

"I know, girl, I need deliverance," Lin said smiling at me. "Okay, go 'head."

"Okay, this was my dream; I saw myself at church, at the altar, saying a prayer: 'Lord, if You just give me a mate, I'll serve You all the days of my life.' Then I turned around and then there was Mark. But, just as quick, he was gone. Then I saw myself standing before God. I didn't actually see God, but I knew that's who I was talking to."

"Girl, this is good. What did God say?" I had Linda's full attention as she leaned forward on the table.

"God asked me why I was so mad at Him. I told Him because He let Mark get away and because I thought we had a deal."

Lin sat back in her chair as I finished telling her my dream.

"Then God said, 'Did Mark come from Me?' And I told God, 'I met him in church.' And just then, a little dude came running up to me and said, kinda hissing, 'Permissive will.' I stood there dumfounded. I didn't understand where I went wrong. Then I woke up. Wasn't that strange? What do you think it means?"

"Mo, God looks at your heart and He knows who and what you need. Just let God have His perfect work in you."

"Isn't that going to take a long time? God's perfect work?" I asked hoping she had the answer.

Linda laughed without actually answering my question. "What'cha doing Friday?"

"Nothing. Why?"

"Come with me to my church. I've grown so much as a woman and as a Christian since being there. I know you'll like it. We throw down." Lin lifted her hands in the air and began to dance right there in her seat.

"Church. On a Friday night?" I said, not believing that anybody in America went to church on a Friday night. My church, well the one I used to go to, only opened its doors twice a week: two Sunday services and a Thursday night Bible study. Other than that, I don't think they ever opened. "I don't know, Linda," I said reservedly.

"Okay, just let me know if you change your mind."

"I will, but first I gotta get ready for my meeting with personnel."

"Call me later and tell me how it went. You know I'm praying," Linda yelled across the cafeteria as I walked into the hallway leading to Human Resources.

~~~~~~~

"Hello. I'm Joyce Leslie, head of personnel, and I will be handling your injury case," the dark skinned lady with grayish hair said as she extended her hand to me. Our handshake was firm but pleasant.

"I'm sorry. I was unaware that I had *a case*," I said while looking around her office, viewing the various awards and certificates she had received.

"I've been in contact with Nurse Guthrey as well as your supervisor, Mr. Walters. Our plan of action for now is to treat your injury and monitor you at your current reassigned position and see how you progress from there. By the way, do you like your new job?"

"So far so good. Mr. Walters seems okay to work for. But what about my day off?" I asked.

"What about it?"

"Well, right now, I don't have one," I explained.

"I understand Fridays are the slowest days in your division. If you're in agreement, Friday can become your day off. You can even begin with this Friday coming up if you want."

"Friday? Cool. Thanks." I looked forward to three-day weekends every week.

"Do you have any more questions?"

"Yes. You said earlier that you would be monitoring my case. For how long?"

"Right now that has not been determined. But rest assured, your position and your salary will not be affected." Ms. Leslie was very professional.

"Thank you. Is that it?" I said while standing up from the plush chair.

"Yes. That's all for today," she said as she swiveled around so I could no longer see her face.

I got back to my desk and reached for the phone book. I flipped through the yellow pages until I found the section I was looking for. The heading read, "Attorneys at Law." I said a quick prayer, "Lord, help me not to pick a fool please." I followed my finger down the page until it stopped. I picked up the phone and dialed.

"Law offices. How may I assist you today?" inquired the young voice on the other line.

"Yes. I have a work-related injury I need to discuss."

"Ma'am, hold on. I'll get one of our best attorneys for you. Can I get your name?"

"Sure you can. My name is Moniqué Clark."

~~~~~~~~

Everything in me wanted to call Mark. It was Friday night and I was bored stiff. Every time I picked up the phone to dial his number, the conversation with Toni popped into my head. Immediately, I would hang up the phone. I still loved Mark and missed him (parts of him) terribly, but I was confused. I wasn't sure *who* it was that I loved.

Momma always said, "If you wanna know what real love is, go to 1 Corinthians 13. It'll tell you everything you need to know." So I picked up my Bible off the stand in the corner, dusted it off and turned to the book of First Corinthians, chapter thirteen, verse four. It said, "*Love is patient and kind. Love is not jealous or boastful or proud or rude. Love does not demand its own way. Love is not irritable, and it keeps no record of when it has been wronged. It is never glad about injustice but rejoices whenever the truth wins out. Love never gives up, never loses faith, is always hopeful, and endures through every circumstance. Love will last forever...."*

"But God," I screamed, overwhelmed and frustrated. "How can I believe in a forever when I can't even get a good year!"

My thoughts were interrupted by the loud ringing of the phone.

"Mo, you and the kids get ready. I'm coming to get'cha. I'll be there in about twenty minutes," Linda insisted.

"Lin, the kids are with Darren. It's his weekend."

"Okay, then I'll come and get you."

"Linda, I'm tired and I really don't feel like going anywhere," I lied. I wasn't tired.

"Mo, I'm not taking no for an answer." And with that, Linda hung up the phone.

Just like she said, Linda Freeman knocked on my front door about twenty minutes later and took me to church.

~~~~~~~~~

"Hey, baby, how you doin'?" the usher at the door asked Linda.

"Baby, I'm doing fine. How you?"

"Blessed and highly-favored," she answered, as Lin and I made our way into the sanctuary.

Exuberance filled the air. The music was pumping. I mean it was loud. I felt the vibration from the bass guitar underneath my feet. The drummer had a serious groove thing going on, and the guy on the piano had those ivories singing. Electricity was in the air and definitely in that place.

Jeans, T-shirts and tennis shoes were the attire of choice. Everywhere I looked there were excited people who smiled and danced in front of their seats. Some actually moved and danced within the aisle. There wasn't a soul who sat down, but then again, with all the activity that went on, who could sit? My mind was cluttered and I didn't believe what I saw with my own two eyes. Was I where I thought I was? The sign on the wall outside read, "First Baptist," but I wasn't in any *church* I had been in before.

The ministry was awesome. The anointing filled the sanctuary. The worship and the praise were real. But it took me awhile to get used to it. When I first walked through the doors, people seemed somewhat strange. Parishioners hugged and kissed each other on the cheeks. People wept and shouted. They sang song after song. It didn't matter if it was fast or slow.

And Linda, she was in her zone. We sat by some of her friends: Michelle, Donna, Janae and Laura. Their mannerisms were similar to everyone else's in the congregation. When they sang, they'd look at each other, point to the sky and shout, "Glory."

I felt weird as I stood there and watched. I probably had my mouth wide open from shock the entire time. Linda tried to reassure me as she held my hand and at times squeezed it ever so gently. She whispered, "It's okay, Moniqué. Do whatever feels comfortable."

I thought to myself, Well, then, I'm out of here. But I couldn't move, especially when the Word was preached. The sermon was both powerful and simplistic at the same time. I borrowed some paper from Linda and took at least three pages of notes.

When we arrived at my apartment, I said to Linda, "Thank you so much for insisting that I come with you tonight. I really enjoyed myself." I reached for the car door handle.

"Oh Mo, you know you're welcome. I enjoyed your company. But, where are you going?" Linda probed me softly.

Unsure of what she meant, I looked at Linda with a questioning expression on my face. "Honey, we have to pray first," she said with that smile of hers.

Not knowing a soul who could resist a smile like that, my shoulders relaxed back into my seat. Linda took my hands and prayed: "*Dear Heavenly Father, I give honor and praise to Your holy and righteous name. I humble myself before You. I thank You for another opportunity and privilege to approach Your throne of grace and receive mercy to help me in the time of need.*

"*Father, I know I don't really know how to pray as I ought, but You told me in Your Word that I am not to lean on my own understanding but I am to trust and acknowledge You in all situations, and then You will direct my path. Well, Father, I do trust You and I acknowledge You as Lord and Master over my life. I know that Your ears are always open to my prayers and that You're listening right now. So, I come to You this time on behalf of my friend, Moniqué.*

"*Father God, You said that I am to make my requests known unto You, so I ask that You meet the needs of this daughter of Yours. I pray, God, that You would restore her joy, and take away the spirit of heaviness and replace it with a spirit of praise.*

"*Father God, touch her heart right now and give her new strength in her inner man. Lord, I pray that she will begin to hunger and thirst for YOU in a greater way than ever before. I pray she will come to know that nothing else will satisfy her like You, my God.*

"*Lord, no one can love her like You can; no one can give her the peace that is only found in You. No one cares for her like You do; no one can lift her and bless her like You can. Father, I pray and ask that You encourage her heart and lift her head once again. Father, You have said that the life of the flesh is in the blood. I plead the blood of Jesus Christ over Moniqué's life. I plead the blood over her mind, her emotions, her body and her will. I pray, God, that You will cause every dead part of her to come alive.*

*"Lord, God, I pray You would help this sister to be reminded of every promise You've already given her in Your Word. I pray she would begin to crave and meditate on Your Word as never before and understand that it is just as important as the air she breathes.*

*"Finally, God, I ask that You help Moniqué, Your child, discover the gift of Your perfect peace You promise to give to all those who keep their minds stayed on You and not on the problems they face. Help her to see, know and understand that You are the problem solver and all she has to do is give her problems to You, trust You to fix it, and then step back and watch You move. Father, thank You for listening to this, my request, and I thank You for Your answer to this request. For You do all things well. In Jesus's name, I pray. Amen."*

Great drops of tears streamed steadily down my face as I looked at Linda in awe. How did she know? How did she capture in just a few short minutes my thoughts and feelings—things I didn't know how to express aloud or to God? I didn't want to spoil or waste a moment of what I felt, so I just reached over to Linda and hugged her really, really tight. I said, "See you Sunday."

Linda's eyes widened.

"Yeah, girl, I gotta bring Nicole and Jordan to that church. They're going to love it."

Linda responded, "All right, now."

As soon as I got in, I called Mark. It was only 9:30.

"Hello?"

"Mark, hey, it's me, Moniqué," I said, surprised he was even at home.

"How are you?"

"Fine. No, I take that back. I'm wonderful."

"Don't you sound excited. What's up, or should I say, who's got you so excited?"

"Now see, I ain't even going there with you. A person can't just call and share some good news with a friend?" I tried to move the conversation forward.

"Oh, so is that what we are nowadays. I ain't talked to you in so long, I thought you fell off the face of the planet." Mark was being facetious.

"Well apparently, the only time you want to talk is when I make the effort to call you," I said and then became very quiet.

"Hello, hello. Are you still there?" he said.

"Yeah, I'm here." I wondered why I was.

"So. Why'd you call this late?"

I paused before answering Mark. I pondered if I wanted to just ignore his previous question and go ahead and share my experience of the night, or just go straight up hand-pointing-head-moving-neck-jerking *sister-girl* on him and fuss him out. I spoke out loud, "It's amazing what tactics the enemy will use, or should I say, who he uses, to steal your joy." The preacher earlier had said the same thing.

"What did you just say?" Mark was insulted as I hit a nerve.

"Oh, you heard me correctly the first time," I snapped. "But like Linda always says, that devil is a lie. You ain't stealing my joy anymore," I declared, not only to Mark, but also to the enemy himself (if he was listening). Again, the preacher earlier had said that the enemy (the devil) can hear you, too, not just God. (I told you I took notes.)

"Oh, so that's who's got you all excited, your friend *Linda,*" he said as he placed an emphasis on Linda's name.

"No, boy. It's not Linda who's got me excited. It's Jesus. You do know Him, don't cha?" I hadn't realized it until the moment the words came out of my mouth. I was excited and it was because of Jesus. Something happened to me in that service that hadn't happened the entire time I went to church with Mark.

"Funny, Moniqué."

"I don't remember getting a call from you tonight. Oh, I must have missed it while I was out." I sighed, took a deep breath and as I exhaled said, "Why do I even bother with you?"

"Why you bother with *me*?" Mark said. "I think you might want to flip the script on that one."

Oh, I know he ain't tryin' to play some mind game on me. Now all of a sudden, this mess is all my fault? were my thoughts as Mark continued to talk.

"Before you start playing the blame game, sister, or get that Miss Holier-than-thou attitude, I suggest you check yourself first." His words were indignant.

## CHAPTER SEVEN

The red light from the clock was so bright against the darkness of the room at five o'clock in the morning. Mark's words echoed in my head as I pressed the play button on my CD player hoping the soft music would lull me back to sleep for the hour I had left before going to work.

"I wish I could tell you what I want...," the song began. A few seconds later I heard, "You said my trials only come to make me strong." By then, my pillow was soaked from my tears as the songwriter had captured in a few short bars what seemed to encompass my life. I wished I could tell God what I wanted. I wished I knew. Turning over, I talked to the ceiling.

"God, what's up with me? One minute I'm flying high in Jesus, and then it seems like the next moment I act like I haven't even heard of Your name. I mean, what's the deal?" The music continued as did I. "God, I feel like a lifeless plant in desperate need of watering. God, I know You know my heart, and God I know You know my needs. Please, Lord, I'm begging You, please fill this void I have deep within me."

My thoughts stopped as I listened to the rest of the song. The words being sung rang like church bells through my soul. It was my testimony. I felt a release in me from the depths of my spirit.

Hollowed out from the core of my belly came His name, "God!" Scripture came from a place beyond me. "Your Word says that *You would never leave me nor forsake me.* God, that's what Your Word says."

Overwhelmed, I got into a fetal position and asked, "God, oh God, where are You? Don't You hear me? Don't You see me?" I looked around the room and nothing changed. There was no sparkling bright light, no thunder or lightning bolt. Nothing.

I guessed God had better plans than to answer little old me. I sobbed, cried and boo-hooed. Call it what you want. It wasn't very pretty or attractive, but it was real.

Suddenly the phone rang. I sniffed and wiped my nose with the sleeve of my gown. Maybe God had heard me after all.

The voice on the other end spoke deeply like I imagined God to sound and said, "I thought you could use a friend."

It was God! I got so excited and screamed, "God."

"You used to call me that," he said.

"Greg?"

"Good Morning. How come you haven't returned any of my calls? I know I mentioned on your machine that it was important that I speak to you."

"I just haven't," I said, disgusted it was him and not God. It was six o'clock in the morning.

"So, how have you been? I've been concerned about you."

"I'm fine, Greg. There's no need for you to be concerned. I made sure that whatever was between us was purposely killed long ago." There was no need to sugarcoat my words for I had had plenty of time to come to terms with what I had done. A part of me still needed to experience the pain.

86

The abortion, my abortion, as far as I was concerned, felt like it happened yesterday....

I was reading the positive results of the home pregnancy kit when Darren walked into our bathroom, the wand still in my hand. Without even asking what the results were, he picked me up and twirled me around the room. Darren loved kids and wanted a lot of them. My eyes filled with tears as my heart was convicted. Darren's ecstatic words resounded over and over in my ears, *"You're pregnant, you're pregnant, you're pregnant!"* His words stayed in my head for the several days I led him to believe the baby I carried in my womb was his.

The days I carried the secret were the worst in my life. I was a nervous wreck. It took everything I had to convince Darren not to tell our family members of the pregnancy. I told him I wanted to make an appointment with my gynecologist first. And then, once he confirmed the results, we could tell the world if Darren wanted. He agreed with me but confessed he didn't like keeping any secrets. I thought I was going to die right there on the spot.

It was during those days that I couldn't eat or sleep. And Darren. He was so nice to me as he fed me crackers and 7Up. He thought I was having morning sickness like I had with Nicole and Jordan.

As agreed, I went to the doctor's and gave a sample of blood and urine. They asked me if I wanted to stay for the results, but I declined. The way my body had rapidly changed, I felt pregnant. They did promise, however, to call me with the results later in the afternoon.

~~~~~~~~

"Mrs. Kennedy?"

"Yes."

"This is Sharon from Dr. Watson's office. How are you today?"

"I'm fine."

"Well, I'm calling because I have your lab results."

"Okay."

"First, congratulations are in order, you are definitely pregnant. We will know just how far along you are on your next appointment. Is next Tuesday, nine-thirty, good for you?"

"Tuesday is fine. Thanks for calling and I will see you then," I said.

"Oh, Mrs. Kennedy, before you hang up. I'm not really sure how to say this but, uh, your lab results also show that you have an STD."

"An STD?" I said lowering my voice to a whisper. "There has to be some kind of mistake. I have never in my life had a STD. Are you sure?"

"Yes, Ma'am. I did the test myself. I'm sure."

I was embarrassed beyond words. I had been a patient at that office since I was a teenager. I knew everybody who worked there.

"Moniqué. I know this is a sensitive subject, but you need to notify your partner or partners of your STD. They need to be tested immediately so they can receive treatment as well."

Darren walked into the kitchen where I was. "Hey baby, you need something?" he said as he reached his head into the refrigerator door.

I shook my head no to him as the nurse continued to talk. "I already took the liberty of calling your pharmacist with the prescription. It's safe to take, and it won't harm your precious baby at all. Just take it for the next ten days and you'll be fine."

"Thanks, Sharon. I'll see you on Tuesday." I spoke confidently. I tried to retain as much of my dignity as possible as I ended our call.

"So who was that on the phone?" Darren asked as he leaned against the kitchen sink, chewing on a piece of celery.

"Nobody."

"If it was nobody, then how come you are going to see them on Tuesday?"

"It was Sharon from Dr. Watson's office."

Darren beamed from ear to ear anticipating their confirmation of my test results.

Briefly, I thought about keeping the baby and rearing it as our own. Nobody would know. But how could I let Darren believe that the baby was his when all along it belonged to someone else? How could I do that to him? I'd have to live a lie the rest of my life. And I wasn't willing to do that. The guilt consumed me.

Darren's eyes were filled with so much joy the moment before I told him about the affair, the baby and the STD. Minutes later, those same eyes were filled with the deepest tears I had ever seen in my life. Darren stormed out of the house. The force of the door slamming shut knocked two pictures off the wall. Our wedding picture was the first to break. Our family picture broke second.

~~~~~~~~

July sixteenth.

"I don't understand why you have to go. And I don't understand why you even want to go," I said placing my sanitary napkins in the small bag.

"How many times do I have to say this, Moniqué. You are still my responsibility. I takes care of mine. Plus, don't nobody else but me and you need to know what's been going on up in here. Do you understand me?" Darren's stare was fierce.

I understood Darren very well. It wasn't like I wanted anyone else to know that I was aborting a baby.

When we got to the doctor's office, I checked in while Darren took a seat in the corner.

"Mrs. Kennedy," the young lady dressed in blue scrubs called my name.

I motioned to Darren to come with me. He shook his head, no.

There were bright lights above as I lay on a gurney atop cool, crisp white sheets. I counted backwards, starting from ten. I don't remember getting to the number nine.

A couple of hours later, the nurse walked me into the doctor's private office. They needed the room I was recovering in for another patient. Resting on a brown leather couch, I stared wildly at the open door. The name in black bold letters read, "Dr. M. Valentine." I glanced around his office and a part of me admired all of the many plaques and distinguished "Doctor of the Year" awards he had hanging in various places around the room. I lay there, however, motionless, waiting for the nurse to give me the release papers. Somewhat out of it, I guess the drugs they pushed so easily through my veins lingered inside me still, I closed my heavy eyes and placed my quivering hands on my flat belly, my womb. The space, now empty, just brief moments before contained something, someone I knew nothing of. It *was* an innocent baby that used to be inside me. But not just any baby, it was the baby I had conceived with Greg. A single tear from my closed eyelid managed to roll down my swollen face at the exact moment Darren entered the room. I'm not sure which emotion, remorse or regret, riveted inside my being to trigger the tear, but I knew somewhere within, I had experienced a loss of great magnitude.

"What are you crying for now? Your butt should have been crying when your unfaithful ass was screwing around on me. It's over now. Come on, get your stuff and let's go!" Darren demanded matter-of-factly, as he pointed to my belongings on the chair next to me. His voice and his glare were void of compassion, love and remorse. The doctors must have felt the same way because before I was totally under anesthetic, I remember hearing one of them remark as well, "*Another* young woman killing *another* baby."

I wasn't mad at Darren, though. His words were spoken out of anger, disappointment and frustration for the dreams and hopes he had for me, for our family. Each time I allowed Greg inside me, I systematically tore apart Darren as well. He just wasn't in the room.

As I walked to the car on that cool summer's day, tender from the outpatient surgery, my mind was a total blank. I felt empty. And I knew that somehow *I* had *changed.* On the way home, Darren told me never to tell Greg about the baby or the abortion. And I never did. But I did forward the bill to Greg. I told the lady at the desk to describe the procedure billed as a "cyst removal." Weeks after the procedure, I called the doctor's office and they told me that the bill had been paid in full with cash.

Darren stayed with me and the kids for about a month afterwards. We argued everyday. And then finally, one day he came home from work, packed his suitcase and placed his house key on the table. He told me that I could have the house and everything it contained. As far as he was concerned, it was all a lie. Darren said that he wanted to be in the kids' lives, but not mine. And as he walked out of the door for the last time, he quipped, "You need to keep your damn legs closed."

I shook my head and refocused on the present phone call. "Why are you calling, Greg?" I asked.

"Well. I've really wanted to call you ever since I heard your voice on Toni's line."

"So, that was you."

"I wanted to say something to you but I couldn't, not in front of my baby."

Everything in me understood what Greg was trying to convey.

"Moniqué, I don't know how to say this, so I'll just say it."

"Say what?"

"Did you have an abortion when we were together? Is that why you just walked away without so much as a good-bye?"

I knew Greg was a smart man and that eventually he would figure things out for himself one day. But I didn't answer him. I remembered Darren's wish, and even though I did not honor our marriage vows, I was determined to honor his last wish as my husband.

"Greg, dear. Let's just leave the past where it belongs, behind us. Forgotten, buried."

"But Moniqué, I still love you." Greg's voice trembled.

"And your wife. Do you still love her, too?"

"Moniqué, you know it's complicated. But yes, I do love her."

"Greg. It's not complicated at all. Love your wife, and please, leave me alone."

"Alone. You want me to leave you alone? How about you dropping that so-called deacon you and my daughter share. You don't seem to mind sharing him, why not me?" Greg said as he revealed his true self.

I hung up on him.

## CHAPTER EIGHT

Hello, Triple A Insurance Company. Moniqué Kennedy. How may I assist you?"

"By coming back into my life. I miss you and I don't want to live without you. Moniqué, forgive me. I've allowed my pride to get the better of me. That's why I haven't called you before now. But God has been dealing with me concerning humility and repentance, and I'm really trying to change. Can you please forgive me, Moniqué?"

My supervisor walked up to my desk. I quickly placed the receiver down.

"Moniqué, you have a meeting with personnel at one o'clock."

"Okay, Mr. Walters," I said as he walked away. I placed the receiver to my ear and said to Mark, "Sorry about that. Now, what were you saying?" I wanted to hear him grovel some more. I needed to hear desperation in his tone.

"Forgive me, Moniqué," he said again in his Barry White tone.

"Mark, this really isn't the best time or place to talk about this. Wouldn't you agree?"

"No, actually I don't. If not now, then when, where? You don't come to church anymore, how am I going to see you?"

My heart sank as I didn't respond.

"Can I come over? Tonight? Please," Mark whined.

~~~~~~~~~

The first few moments were really awkward. Mark walked through the door of my apartment and I didn't know whether to hug him or hit him. The fact that he cheated on me still angered me. He reached out to me, but I moved away, asking instead, "Can I get you something?"

"No, I'm fine," Mark said as he stared at me.

And, yes, he was fine. Aroused, I began to tingle *down south* (if you know what I mean). I had too much nervous energy. Walking around the apartment, I did silly things like water my plants and wipe the kitchen table down.

Mark patted the space on the couch beside him, "Moniqué, sit by me for a minute. I promise, I won't bite."

I threw the dishtowel in the sink and walked over to him. I lost my nerve. "I'm sorry. I can't do this. I thought by now I was ready to talk to you about my real feelings, but…," I said while looking for my car keys and purse. "I need some air. Do you want to take a ride?"

"Moniqué, I'd rather sit here and hold you. I miss you." His eyes seemed sincere.

But I couldn't stay in that house with him a moment longer. I didn't trust him. I didn't trust myself. "I'ma go to the store. I'll be right back. Are you cool here by yourself?"

"Are your kids coming back tonight?"

"No, they're at Darren's."

"In that case, go ahead, I'll be fine. Do you mind if I turn on the TV?"

I handed him the remote from off the top of the TV and told him, "Knock yourself out."

"Hey…take my car," he said as he reached into his pants pocket and lobbed the keys in my direction.

I caught them and said, "O…kay. See you in a minute." I don't know why, but I felt like I owed him something, so I forced myself to give him a kiss on the cheek.

It was a wonderful midsummer night. The humidity lingered in the air as a slight easterly wind crept through the cracked driver's side window. I placed Mark's key into the ignition of his car and drove off. The radio was on. "Hello, my radio listeners out there. This is Bobby J, master of oldies but goodies. Anybody out there want to hear some good stuff? I mean, is there anybody out there who wants to hear some funky stuff? Well, I got the queen of soul and her hit…."

Aretha's award-winning song began to sting parts of me with each word she belted out. Somehow within my spirit, I knew I fit the category of which she sang to a tee. Desperate to change the song, my finger fumbled across the dashboard for another black button. Instead of changing the station, I turned on the heat. Aretha's words continued, *"You got me where you want me, I ain't nothing but your fool, you treated me mean, ah, you treated me cruel."*

I didn't notice, but by the time the song ended, I was parked in front of Mark's house. The porch light called my name, "Monique, come to me." I needed no further encouragement to do what I knew I should not have been doing.

Nervously I fumbled with Mark's key ring in my hand. It took me forever to find his door key. After several unsuccessful tries, eventually I found the correct key and entered Mark's home. Before I locked the front door, I peeked outside to make sure I had no witnesses to my uninvited entry.

Curiosity at almost a dangerous level, I entered the first room on my left. "Quaint, but small for my taste," I thought of the kitchen. Under the scrutiny of a bright light, it looked differently than before. I compared myself with Mark's ex; "She didn't do much cooking, I see. No wonder he eats out all of the time. Boy, if he was my husband...." My thoughts were immediately halted as my eyes caught up with the information my brain had already registered. In the middle of the stainless steel kitchen sink sat two empty Champagne glasses. My mind flashed back to a dinner months before. As Mark and I sat at our table in the restaurant, the host began to read the list of alcoholic beverages. Mark interrupted and Christianly announced for the both of us, "We do not drink."

Evidently some things in Mark's life had change since then. Upon closer examination, one of the glasses had a crimson colored lip mark on the side. Adjacent to the glasses sat a plate with remnants of grapes and strawberries.

As I searched for more clues, the trash can told the entire story. Inside the green, plastic container were Chinese takeout and a bottle of Moet Champagne. (Opened properly, might I add, because the cork was still intact—a little something I learned from a bartender during my partying days.) Also in the trash can (okay, okay, underneath some other stuff because by then I had to dig a little deeper), was a half pint of French vanilla ice cream, the plastic containers for the grapes and strawberries and a dried up red rose. I found the card that had been attached to the rose and tried to read the writing, but juice from something made it unreadable.

Curiosity had now taken a back seat to anger. I threw down what I had found and ran straight back to the bedroom. Visions of the obvious recent activity ran through my mind. I expected the bedroom (okay, the bed), to be in shambles, but it was quite the opposite. The bedroom was immaculate. There didn't seem to be a thing out of place.

A part of me needed more ammunition for the next *Rumble in the Jungle* boxing match that was about to take place at my apartment. Frantic, I searched his bathroom for more evidence.

I combed through his medicine cabinet like I was a forensics specialist called in to examine a murder; I lifted every bandage, razor and fingernail clipper I found. Each object was under the scrutiny of a woman in search of evidence of the *other* woman. As I surveyed each of the three stacked shelves in the medicine cabinet, determined to uncover something, my heart raced with anticipation. After I searched everything I could, my shoulders collapsed from the weight of my emotional heaviness. My steady hand reached for the glass door of the cabinet to close it.

"One last glance," I said to myself.

Nestled on the bottom shelf of the cabinet, hidden to the normal eye, and packaged exactly like an alka-seltzer plus cold tablet, laid an *average size,* Trojan brand condom. I bent down, looked underneath the basin of the sink and found the box. On the front of the package, it read, "Contains 3 latex condoms." There was only one packet in the medicine cabinet and none left in the box.

A cloud loomed over my head and I felt weak to my knees.

Unsure of my footing, I braced myself against the glass shower doors and felt my surroundings for the toilet seat. I sat down to regain my normal breathing pattern. I knew if I kept breathing at my current rate, I would either pass out or die right there on the spot. A single tear fell slowly from my eye. Its presence left a trail of salt residue on my face. I reached down and tore a piece of toilet paper from the roll and wiped my face, when I saw a glimpse of something out of the corner of my eye. I knelt down and extended my hand into the space that separated the toilet from the shower. I reached for the unknown object; it felt soft in my hand.

"It's silk," I thought. The object lay in the center of my palm. "Silk draws," I hollered as I dropped the petite, ladies panties as if they were a dead cat. I immediately washed my hands with soap and hot water. As I stood in the doorway, drying my hands, my eyes focused on the bed—his mattress, in particular. I heard a voice say, "Look under it." So I did. At first I didn't see anything and I started to give a sigh of relief, when all of a sudden, my eyes caught a tiny glimpse of *something* on the opposite side. I walked to the other side of the bed and lifted the heavy mattress with one hand. My adrenaline had kicked in. It wasn't my imagination; it was indeed a white, oblong piece of paper. A letter! It was already opened but that really didn't matter, because knowing myself like I did, I would have opened it anyway. I read the letter. No, I broke the record for speed reading.

The letter stated that this young lady, Brenda, was in love with Mark. She, too, met him at the church, in the new members' class. She said that he made her feel so good about herself and that she was willing to do anything for him. She also wrote that the last couple of months, he made her feel real special, and if he needed anything from her, all he had to do was ask. (Ugh, can I puke now?) Brenda also mentioned that she enjoyed *making love* to him and it was the best experience of her life. Mark, supposedly, was warm, caring and gentle with her. She said, if she were to close her eyes, she could still feel him.

I threw the letter on the floor; I had seen enough. I got Mark's keys off the kitchen table and left. I slammed the door behind me loud enough that Mark probably heard it from my apartment. As I pulled away from the curb, I saw two of Mark's neighbors bolt out of their homes. I smiled with anticipation and said underneath my breath, "You ain't heard nothing yet."

My heart raced faster than the speed on the speedometer as I rushed home. "Boy, you just wait until I get a hold of you," I said angrily as though Mark could hear every word. "I can't believe you got me again. How stupid can I be? But I tell you what, not again," I said as I tried to convince myself into believing my own words.

As I got closer to home, my stomach tightened in fear—in fear of what I knew I was capable of saying and doing when I got angry. I prayed so I would do the right thing.

*"Lord, please help me. Please take this anger from me before I hurt him. Lord, I know I shouldn't have been looking in his house, but I did. Now, what do I do with that information? Lord, is Mark the one You want in my life? Have I brought all of this on myself? Instead of being lovers, are we just supposed to be friends? And if that's the case, then, Lord, why did You bring him into my life? Especially when You knew how much I wanted someone in my life."*

I pulled into the driveway and sat still in the seat, turning off the ignition. I wanted to sit until God Himself spoke the answers to my questions out loud. Again, there was nothing but silence from the stars in the sky, as well as from God.

When I stepped out of the car, Mark emerged from the door grinning. His arms were stretched wide, waiting for me to enter them.

I pushed past Mark in a hurry to reach my bedroom. Kneeling down by the bed, I searched my dresser drawers for the notes I had taken at First Baptist. I hadn't read them since that Friday night, but somehow I knew I would need them later. Apparently, sooner than later. I turned the pages so fast that I almost ripped a couple of them in two. "I know it's in here, I just know it is. Where is it, Lord?" An urgency came through my vocal chords. My hands shook I was so mad. "Ahhh," sighing in relief, I found the Scripture.

With my eyes fixed on the page, I began to read aloud Deuteronomy 1:6-8, *"When we were at Mount Sinai, the LORD our God said to us, 'You have stayed at this mountain long enough. It is time to break camp and move on. Go to the hill country of the Amorites and to all the neighboring regions—the Jordan Valley, the hill country, the western foothills, the Negev, and the coastal plain. Go to the land of the Canaanites and to Lebanon, and all the way to the great Euphrates River. I am giving all this land to you. Go in and occupy it, for it is the land the LORD swore to give to your ancestors Abraham, Isaac, and Jacob, and to all their descendants.' "*

Just as I read the last line, Mark entered the room. He leaned his lengthy body on the edge of the door.

"Moniqué, what's going on?" Mark echoed Marvin Gaye all of a sudden.

Unable to speak a civil word, I rolled my eyes at him as

daringly and belligerently as I knew how. With my Bible Scripture still in hand, I lowered my head and feverishly continued to read my study notes:

*"The city Horeb was literally a burnt and solitude land. After about a year or so there, the people of Israel under the direction of God fixed the place up so that it was suitable for people to dwell there. But after their task had been accomplished (what should have taken them seven days to complete took them forty years), God ordered them to break up their camp at Horeb and enter into their promise land, Canaan—the land that flowed with milk and honey."*

"Excuse me, but you do have company." Mark's insistent words broke my concentration.

Intent on reading the remainder of the highlighted and underlined section of my notes, I ignored Mark's intrusion as he stood in the doorway.

*"When as Christians we go through trials and tribulations, God in His infinite wisdom and mercy knows when our trials and tribulations become more than we can bear. He also knows when we have stayed at the mountain long enough; God will then find the best time to move us on forward in our Christian walk. As a reward, God sets before us a picture or vision of our own promise land, Canaan, as a landmark of encouragement as He commands us to move forward in our Christian course."*

Something on the inside of me quickened as I reread aloud the last part of the Bible study notes for a second time. *He also knows when we have stayed at the mountain long enough...* I felt a strange and unusual surge of strength and motivation. But, I was still mad at the fact that Mark thought he had gotten over on me, once again. Feeling empowered and determined to get his dirt out into the open, I replied to Mark, "Speaking of company, by the looks of things in your house, you've had some recently. Who was it? Toni, or your wife, or somebody totally new, like Brenda?"

Lord have mercy, if there was a sale, I could have bought Mark for a penny. (I probably still would have gotten ripped off.) Mark's eyes popped wide open and his mouth hung in disbelief. Quickly rebounding, however, he said, "My house?"

"I may not practice proper English at all times, but I know I do not have a stuttering problem. But *you* have problems comprehending at times, so I'll repeat myself this once. Yeah, yo house," I had to break-it-on-down for him.

Tension grabbed hold of every molecule in the air.

"But don't sweat the small stuff, honey. Or should I say, don't sweat the fact that I just left your house, seen the Champagne glass with lipstick on it, the red satin drawers in yo bathroom along with yo remaining condom in the medicine cabinet. And, last but not least, the letter under yo mattress."

Mark's eyes were fixed on my fast-moving lips as each word flew out of my mouth. I realized I had given out too much information (I really wanted him to sweat about how much I knew or didn't know), but I said, "The heck with it," and ran with the ball. "Mark, I could handle this situation in a multitude of ways." Standing to my feet, Mark backed away nervously down the short hallway into my living room. Maybe he got a glimpse of my tightly-fisted hands. Following close behind him, I said calmly, "Draws got your tongue?" My head snapped from side to side.

Mark remained composed and silent as he thought of his next move.

Forever the staunch, on display deacon, I thought as I looked at him. Aloud, I said, "I am not going around this mountain again with you," I declared as I handed Mark his car keys and opened the front door for his immediate departure.

Mark took his keys in silence as gloom consumed every pore in his face. Barely above a whisper, Mark said (as though the Scripture he heard earlier in my room had just caught up to him), "Mountain? Is that what I am to you?"

"Mark, you wish you were big as a mountain. But in reality, you're more like a stank, nasty little ditch," I smartly said, placing both of my hands on the center of Mark's chest, shoving him out the door.

Mark stumbled backwards as he lost his footing, but somehow managed to compose himself just milliseconds before falling butt-first onto the sidewalk.

"Damn," I said the moment I closed my door. I quickly corrected the old me and said, "Shoot." I was disappointed he didn't fall on his butt.

I grabbed the phone and dialed the first number that came to mind. I didn't know who would pick up, but that didn't matter, I needed to talk to somebody fast.

The voice on the other line answered with a sluggish tone.

"Why can't I let go? Why do I keep setting myself up for disappointment after disappointment? Am I a glutton for punishment or what?" I whined in disgust of myself.

"Let me guess…old dude, Mark. What's he done this time?"

"Same old mess."

"Well, let's talk about your mess." Shaun said it like he had been waiting for the opportunity to bust me out.

I responded like *Scooby Doo*, "Arrr…ooh."

Shaun went straight into pastor mode.

"Moniqué, there's something on the inside of you that you haven't dealt with yet. And it's called unforgiveness and fear. Let's deal with the unforgiveness issue first."

"Okay." Somewhere deep down inside I knew Shaun was right.

"Have you forgiven yourself for your past, Mo? You know, the things you have alluded to and shared with me. Because God has, you know?"

"I know HE has, but I can't."

"And because you can't or won't forgive yourself, you think and act as if you deserve the mistreatment and lies you get from others. You feel like you need to suffer somehow to be redeemed."

"I do. I've caused so much pain. What I did to Darren ruined everything. I destroyed him, us and an innocent, unborn child in the process. Not to mention the fact that I robbed Nicole and Jordan of a real family home."

"Umm," Shaun moaned and took a deep breath. "Baby girl. Moniqué." Shaun spoke with such empathy. "Jesus died for you. Your debt was, and is, paid in full. There's no other cost but that of discipleship to Jesus Christ."

I shook my head from side to side. I tried to imagine in my mind why Jesus would die for someone like me. He had to have known what and who I was. Yet, I knew in my heart and believed that He did indeed die for *me*. A tear rolled down my face.

"Moniqué, what's your hurry? Why can't you wait on God? For all of your needs," Shaun asked as I remained silent.

"Huh?"

"I'll tell you why. Because when you act out of fear, it will manifest itself in impatience. And faith in God works in the opposite manner. Faith will manifest itself in patience. Psalm 37:7

says, " '*Be still in the presence of the Lord, and wait patiently for Him to act.*' "

I just listened, but not with my ears. I wanted to listen with my heart.

"You're just like the children of Israel. You still got that slave mentality. You're free, but you don't act like it. Because if you did...," Shaun stopped himself.

"Go ahead and say what you were going to saying."

"You haven't had enough yet. You haven't gotten sick and tired of being sick and tired. And until you do, you'll keep going around Mark, oops, I mean the mountain, until you do."

The moment Shaun said "mountain" my mind flashed back to my Bible study notes.

"Don't be like Moses, Moniqué. Because of his disobedience, he was only allowed to *see* the promise land. He never set foot in it. I don't know about you, but I not only want to walk into the promises of God, but I want to possess them as well. Girl, you gonna get me to preachin' up in here."

I smiled.

"The real reason you keep holding on to Mark and all of his baggage is because again, fear is in play, and you're afraid of your tomorrow. You think you're going to be alone for the rest of your life, and that's just not true."

"How do you know I won't be alone for the rest of my life, Shaun?"

"I don't."

"Shaun." I said his name because I didn't know what else to say.

"We serve a God who says it's impossible for you to be alone, especially when He's said He'd be with you always, even to the end of time," Shaun said as he gently corrected me.

"But God ain...."

Shaun wouldn't even let me finish my thought before he interrupted me. "Yeah, I know, go ahead and say it, God ain't a man. If I hear that one mo' time." Shaun was frustrated all of a sudden. He chose his words carefully before he continued, "The Word says that Jesus is God wrapped in flesh, and there is nothing we feel or go through that Jesus didn't or doesn't feel, too."

"But...."

Shaun interrupted me again. "Moniqué, I'ma say this and then I'm through: '*Seek ye first the kingdom of God and His righteousness and all these things shall be added unto you.*' God *has* to be your first priority. He has things He wants to show and give you so that your future will be void of mess and junk, and so He can ultimately use you to be a blessing to someone else."

"Okay, one last question. How will I know when I'm sick and tired?"

"Oh baby, trust me, you'll know. And when you decide to get better by doing better, God's going to show out like never before. Trust me. Trust God. You can take Him at His Word."

"Thank you, Shaun."

"Oh, no, thank you."

"Why?"

"'Cause you just gave me the message for my sermon on Sunday."

"Do you have a title in mind?"

" 'But God,' " Shaun laughed.

"Bye, boy."

"Bye, girrrrl."

## CHAPTER NINE

For a few months, I isolated myself. I went to work, picked up the kids and then went home. The kids asked me several times why we didn't go to church anymore. Especially to the good *church,* they would say. They were talking about First Baptist; they liked the praise dancers and loud music. But the answer I had, I didn't have the nerve to tell them. Nor did I dare tell Shaun or Linda. When Linda asked why she hadn't seen me in church, I lied and told her that I went to the earlier service. And with Shaun, I just didn't return any of his calls.

Over time, I convinced myself that I only got what I deserved. At least, that's what the little voice in my head told me everyday.

Mark cheated and lied on me because I had done the same things to others in the past. Momma always warned me, "Girl, you gonna reap what you sow." And I did. My heart, my ability to trust and my basic desire to care were plowed up and thrown in the trash.

God had to have been disappointed in me. I had failed Him so many times. I no longer prayed. I couldn't. But there were times when I wanted to, when all I wanted to do was talk to God and say, "Lord, I'm sorry. Please, forgive me." I wanted so much to go back to the early days when I was so close with God I even slow danced with the Lord. I wanted to, but…when I knelt down beside my bed and tried, the voice would say things like, "God ain't gonna forgive you." Or, "You know murder is a sin, so is adultery—and with a deacon, no less."

~~~~~~~~

"Moniqué, after church yesterday, Mark made a beeline over to me. What's up with the two of you?" Regina asked.

Although Regina was my sister, I hadn't told anyone but God and Linda about Mark being married. I was too ashamed and felt that I knew better. Saved or not, everyone knows adultery, emotional and physical, is wrong.

"Nothing. You know we don't go together anymore."

"Yeah, that's what I thought. But anyway. He told me that he's been calling you, but you won't return any of his phone calls."

"True. I didn't think we had anything else to talk about. You know how it is," I said, surprised Mark was that desperate to talk to Regina about me and him. Maybe his words of change were real after all.

"Girl, I know. But you didn't see the look in his eyes. Hold on, Nee, for a second."

"Okay."

"Whew, I'm back. Girl, I had to sneeze. Anyway, what was I saying? Oh never mind, I remember. Did you know he was moving to North Carolina? Raleigh, I think he said."

"Naw, I didn't know that. When's he moving?"

"He's gone. He packed up and left right after service. I thought you didn't care," Regina teased.

"I never said that. I *said* we didn't go together."

"I have his number. He asked me to give it to you. It's nine, one, nine...."

Interrupting Regina before she could finish, I said, "Regina, keep it. I don't want it."

"You sure? Oh, I get it, you don't trust yourself, huh?"

"Hey, I gotta go. Ms. Leslie from personnel is walking over here." I tried to look busy since I was at work.

"Oh, okay, bye," Regina said as she hurried off the phone.

~~~~~~~~~

"Hello, Moniqué. Can you step into my office for a minute?"

"Now?" I looked down as the lights blinked on my reception board.

"Yes. Now," Ms. Leslie said as her tone became forceful.

Placing my phone on forward, I followed Ms. Leslie down the long corridor. As she passed her office, she told her secretary, "Please hold all of my calls and advise Ms. Kennedy's supervisor of her whereabouts."

I sat in the first chair available in the large, opulent conference room.

"Can I get you something?" Ms. Leslie asked politely.

"No, thank you. What's this all about?" I wanted to get to the nitty-gritty since she decided to have this impromptu meeting.

"Well, Moniqué, since our last meeting, we have been monitoring your injury for a while now and we feel...."

"We who?" I said defensively, interrupting her.

"Mr. Walters, myself and our higher headquarters."

"Okay...."

"Well, we feel you're ready for a change in position, and with that will come a change in salary as well."

"Oh, really?" I said tapping the antique conference table with my fingernails.

"Moniqué. The company has been gracious and more than accommodating to you and your injury. Normally, the recoup time is only thirty days, and as you well know, you have far exceeded that limit."

"And as you know, Joyce, as do I, if you had a legal leg to stand on, you would have fired me by now. But since you haven't…," I stopped, giving her one of my sister-don't-you-mess-with-me-I-got-a-darn-good-attorney stares. I had her and the company over a barrel and they knew it.

Ms. Leslie was uncomfortable as she pulled on her St. John jacket. "Well, let's just see how this goes for a while, and if this doesn't work out, we can always come back to the table and view other options."

"What other options?" I pressed the issue so I could advise my attorney.

"There's really no need now getting into all of that. Here is the proposed position change, view it, and I expect your final decision in three days." Ms. Leslie pushed the white piece of paper over to my side of the table and excused herself.

"Great," I said walking out of her office, pulling on my suit that I, too, was proud to wear.

Nicole and Jordan flashed across my mind. With a salary cut, some things would have to change. Then I thought of Darren. "Oh, no. I refuse to ask him for one penny more. If I have to, I'll get another job."

Suddenly, the weight of the world was on my shoulders. I

summed up my life in about a minute: pending job change, assured salary decrease, two dependent kids, clothes, daycare costs, food, apartment, light bill, car note and insurance, didn't go to church, convinced God was mad at me, had no friends, ex-husband couldn't stand my guts, and to top it off, the man I loved was married and cheating on me! Could things get any worse or what?

That was the straw that broke the camel's back. I had had enough. I got back to my desk and called my sister.

"Regina. Can I get that number?"

"What number, Moniqué?"

"Regina, don't play with me. I am not in the mood." I pulled the big sister act on her.

"Okay. You gotta pen?"

~~~~~~~~

The phone rang a couple of times before Mark answered. "Hey, dude, what's up with you?" I said as if we hadn't broken up.

"Not much," Mark said. He spoke as if he was unsure of who he was speaking to.

"Do you know who you're talking to?" I asked.

"Moniqué?" He still wasn't sure.

"Yeah, it's me. How are you doing?"

"Better, now that I get a chance to hear your voice and not a damn machine," Mark said.

"Well, that's why I'm calling. What are you doing this weekend? I was thinking we could get together. You're in Raleigh, right?" I said ignoring his attitude.

"Yeah, sure, this weekend would be great," Mark accepted,

but I could tell he was skeptical.

"Okay, it's a date. I'll make all of the arrangements. Can I call you later with the details?"

Before Mark had a chance to respond, my phone beeped. "Hold on a sec," I said clicking over.

"Hello."

"Hey, Moniqué. What's up, this is Troi. I got a question for ya."

"All right," I replied.

"Are you interested in a blind date with a wonderful man?" Troi asked, sounding like a live personal ad.

"Is this a trick question or what? Who in their right mind doesn't want to meet a wonderful man?"

"That's what I thought, so I called you. My husband, William, just got off the phone with a high school friend of his in Raleigh, and he's available. But I tell you right now, he won't be for long."

"Girl, I ain't going on no blind date," but then I asked, "What does he look like?"

"Fine. Built. Smart. Friendly." She fired attributes like bullets in a gun.

"Ooh, Troi, hold on for a minute, I forgot I had someone on the other line."

"Mark?" I hoped he was still on the phone.

"Yeah, I'm still here."

"Look, I need to take this call. I'll call you back later, okay?"

"Promise?" he said, as he sounded almost desperate.

"I promise." I clicked back over to Troi.

"Troi, I'm back."

"Moniqué, on the real tip, I think you and Frank would really make a good couple. He's really nice and you're really nice and…"

"Okay, give him my number," I said talking over her.

"Girl, he's home right now waiting for you to call him."

"Get out of here."

"I told you, he won't be on the market for long. Like MC Hammer, you better bust that move," Troi laughed at herself as she gave me his number. Troi must be the only person on the planet still talking about MC Hammer.

"Troi, you said he lived in Raleigh? North Carolina?"

"Yeah, why?"

"Well, it's funny, but I was thinking about going down there this weekend."

"Oh, my God. That would be perfect. You have to meet him, and he lives right there. Ooh, I feel a love connection," Troi's voice dragged out in her excitement. "Do you want me to set it up for you?"

"Naw. I got a few things I need to work out first." The wheels in my head turned fast. How could I see Mark and this Frank guy, too, in the same weekend?

"Okay. But I'll leave you with my Grandmother's famous words, 'You think long, you think wrong,'" Troi said as she hung up the phone.

"Troi," I yelled through the phone hoping she hadn't hung up yet.

"Yeah," Troi said as she heard my scream.

"Troi, why are you pushing this? Especially with me?"

"I really can't explain it. I just got a feeling you and Frank are meant for each other. I think nice people deserve a chance at love. Maybe it's just the hopeless romantic in me. I don't know."

After Troi hung up, I commented, "Love. Huh. What's that?"

I turned and reached for the remote control to the TV when

my phone rang again.

"Hello?" I said as I thought, is this grand central station or what?

"Moniqué. This is William Shands. How are you this evening?"

William was always so formal in his speech. His voice was deep and quite manly sounding. He had one of those voices you hear on the radio late at night.

"I'm fine," I said smiling at the couple's back-to-back phone calls.

"I don't know what Troi has told you, but let me fill you in on my perspective."

"Should I sit down?"

"No, it's not like that, woman."

"Just checking, because you sound so serious."

With a deep breath William said, "He's in the military. He has a son. He's getting divorced...."

My ears couldn't get past *getting divorced.*" "Excuse me. He's still married?"

"Technically. But let me tell you this."

"I don't want to hear it." Just the thought of going back down that road made me mad.

"Hold up, hear me out first before you make a decision you might regret."

William waited for me to say something, but I didn't.

"In all of my life, I haven't met a man like Frank. He's a good man, and I have the utmost respect for him. His integrity is beyond reproach."

"Reproach, huh. Well, is he saved? Gay? Is he a smoker? Does he own his own car? How's his credit?" I rolled the questions off my tongue with ease.

"Where in the world did the gay question come from?" William said, as if that was the only question that was asked.

"William, I just finished reading this book, and to make a long story short, believe me, it's a question that every woman, and I do mean every woman, in America needs to ask. Do you realize who's getting AIDS nowadays? It's us women. The latest study as of last year said that new adult, adolescent HIV infections among women worldwide is almost fifty percent. Men live secret lives—gay, married, bi—and we pay the cost, the ultimate cost, for it." I had gotten on my soapbox and William knew it.

"Okay, okay. I'll leave that alone, but to my knowledge, the answer is no, he's not gay. And to set the record straight, all men ain't living secret lives. There are men like me, and Frank, who live our lives according to the Word of God."

"Enough said. I'm sold."

"Well, he is, too," William said with laughter in his tone.

"What?"

"I was on the other line talking to him while you were talking to Troi. I had to answer the same kinds of questions about you." William coughed as he tried unsuccessfully to hold back his laughter.

"What did he ask you about me?"

"Well, frankly, no pun intended, he wanted to know what was wrong with you."

"Excuse me?" Jumping to my feet, I placed my hands on my wide hips.

"C'mon now…Before you start jerking your head and waving your hands in the air, let me explain. I told Frank how attractive and intelligent you are, and reasonably so, he wanted to know why you didn't already have a man?"

"Oh," I replied, sinking back onto my bed. "Thanks, William."

"You are very much welcome, Moniqué. Now, call the brother. He's waiting."

I stared at the telephone and searched my mind for the right first words to say. I cleared my throat, "Um, um." I wanted, needed, to sound just right. Alluring, sophisticated, educated and beautiful. I caught a glimpse of myself in the mirror. Talk about uptight, I looked so stiff.

I felt like an idiot as I pumped myself up, "Suck it up, girl. Pick up the phone and call that man. It's not going to kill you; it's just a phone call. You've had millions of phone calls; this one shouldn't be any different. Go ahead," I continued talking to myself, "What am I going to say? I know nothing about him except secondhand information, and how reliable can that really be?" I said aloud as if someone beside me was going to answer my questions.

I imagined the phone call and the eerie sound of nothingness. That all too familiar sound you hear when no one has anything to say to the other person. Uncomfortable seconds pass, while both of you think of something clever and intelligent to say to impress the other. That sound.

I took a long, deep breath and slowly dialed the number. One, nine, one, nine, seven, nine, six,…The phone rang three times. "Maybe he had an errand to run. Maybe he got tired of waiting," I thought. I allowed the phone to ring a fourth time when I heard:

"Hello?" the proper voice said almost in a rush.

"Hello, Frank? This is Moniqué, Troi's friend."

For the life of me, after those few simple words came out of my mouth, I literally had nothing else to say. I froze and felt like a clown. I closed my eyes and imagined myself as the main attraction at the local circus. I saw myself in a big red nose, multicolored wig and long, wide shoes.

"Oh my God," I thought, "What have I gotten myself into? He's probably going to call William and cuss him out for setting him up with a fool."

Like a knight that rode to my rescue, Frank took over the conversation with great ease and comfortability. "Hey, Moniqué. How are you? William and Troi told me a lot about you. I hear you're coming to my city? Have you been here before?"

"Actually, this will be my first time," I said as I looked at myself pace in front of the mirror.

"Do you need directions? I can give them to you if you'd like," Frank asked.

"Thanks, but I think I got that covered." I smiled as I pictured him as a friendly travel agent. I commented to myself how at ease Frank made me feel. Frank spoke as if he had known me all of our lives. Pleasantly taken aback, I continued to look at myself in the mirror. As the conversation continued in duration, my body language told the story. I had relinquished my arm-folded stance at the mirror and now lay on the imaginary sandy beaches of the Bahamas, otherwise known as my bed. I gazed at the ceiling as I tried to imagine his face. Did he look as wonderful as he sounded? Did his eyes reflect the boyish charm in his calming voice? I was surprised at how content, comfortable and relaxed I felt with a stranger. Never before had I felt that way, especially over the telephone. All of a sudden, I felt out of control, so I reeled myself back in from my brief but wonderful retreat.

I thought, "C'mon, Moniqué. It's just *one* phone call. Get a grip, girl. After all, Frank could still be ugly." Hey, things like that matter. Momma always said, "Why should I want someone who nobody else wants?"

"So what brings you to Raleigh?" Frank asked innocently enough.

I swallowed hard. "Huh…Excuse me," I managed to get out of my mouth before I choked.

"Why are you coming to town? Is it business or for fun? Frank rephrased his question.

"Yeah, in a way. There's some old business I have to settle." I told a half-truth as I thought of Mark.

"I would like to take you to lunch, if you have the time"

"I'm sure I can squeeze you in," I smiled as my thoughts turned risqué all of a sudden.

"Let me give you my work number. Call me when you get in town and we can decide then. Ask for Captain Thompson when you call. Only a few people know me by my first name."

I got a pen, wrote down Frank's number, and told him, "I look forward to meeting you, Frank Thompson."

"I am looking forward to meeting you, too. You have a blessed night."

"Blessed." I liked that word a lot. "You, too. Good night," I said as we got off the phone. I took a quick look at myself in the mirror. I beamed. And, if I wasn't mistaken, I thought I caught a glimpse of a sparkle behind my eyes as well.

## CHAPTER TEN

I hated calling Darren to ask him for *anything*. But I needed to switch my weekend with the kids with his. I was hoping he wouldn't give me a hard time about it, but I was prepared nonetheless. I had already called Steph and asked if she would be my backup plan just in case, and she said she would. So I called Darren, but instead of talking to him directly, I had to leave a message on his machine, which frustrated me even more. I'd have to wait for an answer, when and if he decided to call me back. He was in control, and I really hated that. Since our divorce, I was used to handling my business on my own terms.

Relaxing in the tub, I heard the phone, so I jumped out sopping wet.

"Hello."

"It's Darren. I got your message. What do you want?"

"I wanted to know if you can keep the kids this weekend?"

"I just had them."

"I know, but I need to go out of town."

"Why?" Darren asked.

I paused as I thought about telling him the truth or telling a lie. I must have waited too long, because Darren figured it out for himself.

"Oh, I get it. You're going to meet some knucklehead. Oh, hell, no."

"Darren…," I began to say, but he interrupted me.

"I got plans, too. Sorry. I guess you'll have to cancel," he said with a smirk in his tone and hung up.

As I stepped back into the tub filled with bubbles and really hot water, I finished what I was about to say to him, "Darren, I don't need you."

~~~~~~~~~

After the agenda for the weekend was finalized, I called Mark. My plan was to spend Friday and Saturday night with Mark and leave Sunday (after I left Mark) open for Frank. The plan was doable, I thought.

With directions to the hotel in hand, I got on the road. At first, the drive was really nice. I listened to my girl, Aretha. Boy, did she sing. However, I got so wrapped up into her singing that I stopped paying attention to my directions. With one missed exit, I wound up in Wilmington, NC, not Raleigh. Hotter than the demons in hell, I arrived at the hotel in Raleigh, three hours later than planned.

I pulled into the parking lot and gave a sigh of relief. And for a brief minute, I rethought my reason for being there. "Moniqué, are you sure you want to go through with this?" I asked myself. As I opened the door, my mind was made up. I got out of the car, grabbed my bags from the back seat and headed straight for the check-in counter.

"Hi, I'd like to check in. My name is Moniqué…."

"Kennedy," said Mark as he stood behind me, completing my last name for me.

I turned around, shocked to see him. My hope was that he hadn't arrived yet. My fantasy grand entrance was ruined. I had imagined that as I saw him for the first time in months, I'd look good and smell even better. I had gone over in my mind many times on the drive down where exactly I would place the perfume on my body. I wanted Mark to salivate at the mouth…I wanted him to see with his eyes, feel with his hands and taste with his lips what he missed. Instead, when we met, I was dressed in sweats and a T-shirt. I was tired and just a little funky from my long, hot drive.

Stepping back, I got a good look at him, as Mark did at the sight of me. Still visibly upset about my trip down, Mark read the expression on my face. "Moniqué, do you want to sit over here for a minute before going up to the room?" Mark pointed to a couch in the lobby.

I didn't say a word at first. Then I said, "No, let's just go to the room."

Mark pulled me in closer to him as he gave me a tight hug and whispered in my ear, "It is sooo nice to see you, Moniqué."

I reciprocated, but it wasn't a hug, hug. It was one of those hugs you get from people who just lean forward a bit and pat you on your back three times. Mark grabbed my luggage and we walked to the elevator. We were in room 222.

Giving the room a quick once-over, I noticed that Mark had already unpacked his toiletries and put away his clothes for the weekend. I felt like my legs were about to give out, so I walked over and collapsed on the bed. The sheets were cool as was the room. I reached for one of the king-size pillows and melted into it like cotton candy. Mark had drawn the curtains and soft jazz played in the background. Four scented candles burned on the end table adjacent to the bed.

"Moniqué, I'll give you a minute to unwind. I'm going to get some ice. Can I get you anything while I'm out?" Mark was being overly thoughtful.

"No, thank you," I said barely above a whisper.

Mark bent down and gently kissed me on the forehead. I closed my eyes as he walked away. When the door shut, my body dissolved like ice. I allowed my mind to soak in the relaxed atmosphere, until a sharp pain ran through my chest. I rose up quickly...Frank! Flashbacks of our conversation flooded my memory. I was supposed to call him when I got into town.

"Great impression, Moniqué. Way to go," were my immediate thoughts. Oh, my God, what am I going to do? I sat on the bed as the wheels in my head turned. "How am I going to call Frank? I can't do it now. Mark's gonna be back any minute. The ice machine ain't but twenty feet from here. Oh Lord, oh Lord."

I wrecked my brain for an excuse to leave the room once Mark returned. I knew I wasn't too good at lying to his face, but as long as I didn't look him directly in the eyes, I'd be able to get away with it. Plus, he was so glad to see me, I could have probably asked for anything.

When Mark came back into the room, I was still trying to get my lie straight in my head. I rehearsed it so it would come out right.

He smiled at me as he placed the bucket of ice on the table. I smiled back. I waited until Mark faced me to make my move. I sashayed up to him and gave him a big hug around his neck.

"Mmmm," Mark moaned with pleasure.

124

I walked backward as I pulled him closer toward the bed.

"Oh, Moniqué, I can't believe this," he said as he wrapped his long arms around me.

"What?" Like I didn't know what he was talking about. Playfully, I pushed him onto the bed.

"Me and you here," Mark moved his hands to my hips as I climbed on top of him.

"Believe it," I said as I grabbed his face and looked him in the eye. I had begun the first part of my lie. "Hey…why don't you relax while I go get the rest of my stuff out of the car?" I said lifting myself off him and standing in front of the bed. Parts of him were aroused.

"You didn't bring it all in?" he said as his tone grew impatient. Mark held his hands out to me. "Oh no, Moniqué. I can't let you go now. I thought I had lost you forever."

"Ahhh," I said like I had viewed a newborn baby for the first time. But in my head I said, "Ahhh," like when a puppy poops on your white carpet. It was clear that I wasn't going to get away easily.

Just then, the phone rang. Mark and I both looked at each other puzzled. We said at the same time, "It's not for me."

I answered the phone, "Yes. Okay. I'll be right down." It was the wrong number, but Mark didn't know that. I grabbed my purse and ran toward the door. Mark yelled something, but I didn't pay attention to a word he said. In a hurry, I took the stairs. Swinging the door to the lobby open, I searched for a quiet area so I could have some privacy. I reached into my purse for the piece of paper with Frank's telephone numbers. I found it and called him on my cell.

"Can I *please* speak to Captain Frank Thompson?"

"I'm sorry, he's left for the day. Care to leave a message?"

"No, thank you. I'll try his home number." My heart sank in desperation. Quickly, I dialed his home phone. I whispered as the phone rang, "Please be there, please be there." I looked over my shoulder because I thought I saw someone.

"Hello," Frank answered.

"Frank, hi, this is Moniqué."

"Hey, Moniqué, did you make it to Raleigh all right?"

"Yeah, but I made a three hour detour on the way."

"What?"

"Yeah, I went to Wilmington."

"Oh, man, you must've missed your turn," Frank chuckled. "I know you're down here on business. Do you have any time in your schedule where you and I can actually see each other and get something to eat?"

"Uh…Sunday I'm completely free," I said looking over my shoulder again.

"Sunday's cool. We can meet right after I get out of church. How about one o'clock at the mall?"

"Okay, I'll see you on Sunday," I said relieved.

"Sounds like a plan, take care."

I reluctantly closed the lid to my cell. I wanted to meet Frank then more than ever. There was just something in his voice that called to me. Everything inside me screamed, "Frank."

"What have I gotten myself into?" I thought, pressing the second floor button on the elevator wall. I knew that I had to somehow ignore the scream within my heart and listen to the whimper that whispered in my ear, "Mark's waiting for you."

When I entered the room, Mark was gone but had left a note on the pillow. *Be back in a minute—had to check on something,* the note read.

Dropping the note into the trash can, I closed my eyes and stretched across the bed.

~~~~~~~~

"Hey, sleepy head," Mark said to me as he shook my shoulder. "Are you hungry? I am," he said reaching down and grabbing the phone book. "What do you feel like eating tonight?"

"I don't know. You decide," I said, before I yawned.

"How about we just jump in the car and decide on the way?" Mark suggested.

"Can I freshen up first?" I said lifting and smelling underneath my arms.

"Where your bags? Didn't you go to the car?" Mark was looking around the room.

I pretended like I didn't hear him as I walked into the bathroom, closing the door behind me.

Mark and I decided on Chinese. He found a quaint restaurant right off the highway, not too far from the hotel. We sat close to one another and held hands. We sort of felt each other out as we tried to establish comfortable boundaries. We made small talk and tried not to bring up our checkered past. Mark told me repeatedly how special that weekend was for him. I lied and said the same. I didn't have the nerve to tell him the truth. Whatever that was. I didn't know why I was there. I didn't know what it was about Mark that kept me going back to him. I just didn't know. I wish I did.

~~~~~~~~

The next morning, Mark and I had breakfast in the hotel restaurant.

"Moniqué, will you marry me?" he asked with his mouth stuffed with eggs.

Orange juice flew out of my mouth.

"Man, I didn't expect that reaction," Mark said as he halfway smiled.

"Are you serious?"

"Maybe," he said as he continued to eat his breakfast and some of mine.

"In that case, naw boy," I said as I picked up my toast, put it into my mouth and chewed.

"How you gonna dismiss a brother like that?"

"Easy, because we both know you ain't serious, and even if you were, my answer would still be the same. No."

Mark folded his arms across his chest acting like what I said insulted him or something. He sat back in the chair and pouted his lips like a two-year-old.

"Can we please change the subject and eat our breakfast?" I said ignoring his body language.

"Yeah, let's do that." Mark stroked the top of my hand.

The rest of the day was spent sight-seeing. We walked the mall and various other shops. Then around dusk, Mark and I drove out to the countryside and parked by a lake. He had a blanket in his trunk that we used to relax on. Mark gathered rocks for us to toss into the water. As the sun set beneath the horizon, we made love under the cover of moonlight. Mark was very gentle with me and I with him. Our moments were tender and slow. Neither of us made any promises of a tomorrow to the other. As I gathered my things, a half-clothed Mark walked off into bushes. He returned holding a small bunch of wild flowers. A single tear rolled down my face, but I quickly wiped it away before Mark saw it. It was the first tear I had shed since our breakup. That night, in the bed, I tossed and he turned. Neither of us got any sleep, but we both pretended to.

~~~~~~~~

It was Sunday morning, and I was ready to go home.

Silently, Mark and I strolled hand-in-hand to my car after we paid the hotel bill. The summer's breeze hit my bare shoulders and made the tiny hair on my back stand at attention. Mark walked with his head hung low as if he looked for a lost object. Maybe he looked for our relationship. Maybe he looked for my heart.

Mark stopped abruptly and took me by the arm. As I dropped my bags down onto the concrete pavement, Mark held me tightly. At first, my gut reaction was to pull away, but I didn't, I couldn't. I searched for a reason to hold on—to him, to the relationship. In that brief moment, I wanted some kind of sign to tell me if he was really out of my system. Mark continued his grasp on me. I could tell by the way he held me that he didn't want to let go. I pushed him away as his hold on me was broken. I wanted so badly to feel something, anything…but I didn't. At that moment, I was void of any kind of true feelings for him.

"Moniqué, this is the last time I'm going to see you, isn't it?" His eyes spoke louder than his words.

I braced myself as I looked back at him. I remembered how he made me feel the first time I ever saw him. I smiled.

For a brief moment, Mark lit up like the Christmas tree on display at the famous Rockefeller Center in New York City.

Quietly behind us walked a couple. Mark interrupted them, "Excuse me. Do you mind taking a picture of me and my friend here?" he asked as he handed them his camera.

Pressured into it, the man agreed to take our picture. Mark put his hand around my waist, leaned into me and put his chin on top of my head. He said, "Smile, Moniqué. This is one for the history books."

"Cheeeeese," we said together.

The polite stranger took our picture and handed Mark back his camera. We thanked him.

I think Mark knew, just as I did.

I got onto my tiptoes and kissed Mark lightly on the lips. Mark returned my kiss with one to my forehead.

"Mark, I really do have to go."

"I know. But you never did answer my question."

I lowered my head and bit my lip.

"Moniqué. I am so sorry. And I'm not saying that because this is the last time I'm going to see you."

I looked up at him.

"I'm saying it because it's true. From the bottom of my heart. I've also decided to step down as a deacon—need to reevaluate some things. I hope you'll find it in your heart to pray for me sometime."

"Of course I will," I lied.

"Good. And Moniqué."

"Yeah."

"Have fun on your lunch date." Mark winked and walked away.

My face must have cracked into a million pieces as I walked to the car speechless. Sitting down I caught a glimpse of myself in the rearview mirror. "Who in the world?" I wondered. The face looked familiar, but the person behind the eyes had changed. My conscience attacked me. I wanted to rewind time back to the moment when Mark asked me, "Moniqué, was this weekend special for you?"

In my mind, I gave myself a second chance, and that time I told him the truth, "No, it wasn't special. I came with one purpose in mind and that was to make you feel loved and then rip your heart out. I wanted to hurt you like you hurt me." Then I thought about when we were in bed together and Mark asked, "Moniqué, do you still love me?" I should have told him the truth and said, "No."

For the longest time, I called Mark a dog, with a capital D. A low-down, dirty, stank, nasty dog. Because in my heart, he had committed the ultimate crime of deception against me. He perpetrated one thing in public and lived contrary to it in private. His actions were inconsistent with his words.

But then, all of that seemed to pale in comparison with what I saw in myself. I had become who I accused Mark of being—a deceiver, a liar and a fraud. That revelation shook me to my foundation. I was my worst nightmare—him.

I threw the uncomfortable, raw thoughts out of my head as I looked at the clock on my dashboard. It was time for my date with Frank. Again I looked in the mirror, but this time for a different reason. I wanted to make sure my makeup was all right. Frank and I were to meet at the mall, which was right across the street from the hotel.

My face was fine. "I look okay," I said to myself. "After all, I'm not that ugly—at least not on the exterior, that is...the interior part of me might need a second opinion, though."

## CHAPTER ELEVEN

The awesome beauty of the day seized my attention. The sun shined brightly as I tried to see the faces behind the glared windshields of cars as they passed by. Never one to be late, I waited at the red light impatiently. I tapped the top of the steering wheel with the tips of my nails while I read the street sign on the corner. It read, "Crossroads Lane." The light turned green and I drove up the ramp into the parking lot of the mall. I had arrived ahead of time. I was anxious as I waited silently in the car. Every few seconds or so I glanced down at the clock on the dashboard, disappointed because it moved too slow for me. I wanted to meet the man that had my curiosity peeked. As I tried to get my mind off the time, I resumed my watch of the various people who made their way into the Crabtree Valley Mall. At first glance of any man, I wondered if it was Frank.

Patience never being a virtue of mine, I decided to wait for Frank at the entrance of the mall by Ruby Tuesday. But just as I reached for the door handle, a silver car passed by me with a very distinctive looking man inside. My spirit quickened. "It's him," a voice whispered deep inside me.

133

I gathered my purse and confidently walked toward the silver car now parked only five cars down from mine. As I approached the stranger and his car, I knew it was Frank. He sat in his car, looking into the mirror as he readied himself. I smiled because I thought only women did that kind of stuff before a date. Frank closed his car door and walked toward the mall, oblivious to my presence. My timing was perfect as I approached him.

"Excuse me, are you Frank?"

"I sure am," he said.

We smiled together. And I was certain I heard angels singing.

"Hi, I'm Moniqué," I said offering my hand.

"Nice to finally meet you, Moniqué," Frank responded as he took hold of my hand and politely wrapped it around his arm. He extended his other hand to point the way to the restaurant.

I wondered if Frank questioned how I recognized him without me ever seeing a picture of him before. I was relieved that he didn't ask, because I had no logical answer to give him. I just knew it was him when I saw him.

"Is Ruby Tuesday okay with you?"

"Sure. It's one of my favorite restaurants," I responded to Frank's question.

"Why don't you have a seat and I'll get us a table," Frank said as he ushered me to the chair against the restaurant wall.

Right away, I didn't want to gawk or be too obvious, but, I noticed that Frank was rather, shall I say, attractive. No, forget that. My basic primal instincts took over. To say that Frank was merely attractive would be an understatement. Frank was off the chain. He had it *going on*. (That's what Nicole would have said.) Troi mentioned that he was muscular. But when she said that, I pictured in my head the body building type guys. You know the type, muscles bulging out of every pore in their bodies. As Frank stood in front of the podium, putting our names on the list, I quickly threw that image out. Frank was as handsome as he was fit. The black body shirt he had on worked his abs, his chest and his biceps. I chuckled as I imagined myself cuddled up to Frank on a brisk winter's night, up in the Alps somewhere. Okay, okay, back to reality.

With the black square beeper in hand, Frank walked over to me. "Moniqué, it'll be about five minutes. You don't mind, do you?" Frank asked courteously.

"That's okay," I said, but I thought, Boy, I'd wait forever for you.

The hostess spoiled my fantasy moment and called his name, "Thompson. Party of two."

"That's us," Frank said as he held out his arm to me. "I guess this thing doesn't work," Frank said as he handed the beeper back to the hostess.

Seated across from each other, we busied ourselves with the menu. My stomach was nervous and I had a hard time concentrating on the list of options. I looked over at Frank and he had already placed his down on the table. "You're ready to order already?"

"Yeah, I've been here a few times and I pretty much know what I like on the menu." He smiled bashfully. "But take your time. I'm enjoying the view," he said, clearly talking about me.

I blushed as I batted my eyes. "So how was church?"

"It was fine. I really like my church. If I had thought about it sooner, I would have invited you to go with me."

"Maybe some other time. So, are you saved?"

"Yeah, are you?"

"Uh, huh," I said as the waiter brought over our drinks and we ordered our food.

"I'll have the broiled fish with a loaded baked potato, sour cream and butter, the vegetable medley and bread, please," I said as I looked at Frank, giving him the chance to order.

"Yes, give me the grilled chicken with rice and steamed vegetables, please," Frank said matter-of-factly as he reached for my menu and handed both of them to the waiter.

"Is that it? That's all you're going to eat?"

"I had a big breakfast," Frank said as he rubbed his flat stomach.

"I thought about eating a salad...."

"Do you want me to get the waiter back for you?" Frank said as he looked around for the waiter.

"No, no. I said I *thought* about it, but then I heard my stomach growl."

"Well, I'm glad you ordered what you actually wanted."

"Yeah, me, too," I said as I momentarily took my attention off Frank and looked at the pictures on the walls.

"So, how'd your business go?"

Frank's question got my attention quick. Man, I didn't want to have to lie to him. He seemed so genuine. Frank gave off the vibe of the kid in high school everyone liked. He was just as William said. But I couldn't very well tell him the truth, now could I?

"Uh...fine. You know business," I said.

"So was it worth the trip?" he asked.

As I looked at Frank, I answered, "Oh, yes. It was definitely worth it."

"So, what time are you trying to get back home today?"

"Sometime before dark."

"Why before dark?" Frank looked puzzled.

"Because I'm really not a long-distance driver and I don't like driving at night."

"Three hours is long distance to you?"

"Man, yes. Shoot, anything over four hours and I'm taking a plane."

Frank and I laughed together. Our food came and we ate. Every now and again we made eye contact and smiled. Our conversation continued.

"Would you like to go do something after we eat?" Frank had my complete attention as he continued, "Have you ever been to downtown Raleigh? There's a nice museum there that we could go see. It won't take long," Frank said as he was three quarters through with his food.

"Sure, I'd like that. I love museums." I thought, "Mmm mmm. A man with culture, some diversity."

"Great, let me get the bill." Frank motioned to the waiter for the check.

"I'll be right back. Let me go to the ladies' room and then we can go," I said as I excused myself.

I walked away from the table and just knew I'd feel heat rays on my butt. But I didn't. It may have been because Frank wasn't looking, or it may have been that for the first time in a really, really long time, I wouldn't have minded if he did look. Either way, I felt good and I felt good about Frank. Just as it was on the phone, so it was in person. Frank made me feel very comfortable and safe.

~~~~~~~~

Frank and I drove our own cars to the museums. My plan was to leave and get on the road from there.

I parked beside Frank in front of the city's historical museum. Since it was Sunday, we parked for free. He politely walked over to my car and opened my door for me. "A Southern Gentleman," I thought. I was so impressed at his desire to take me to a museum. I had always wanted to go but just chose the wrong men to go with. I wanted that experience to be different. I thought, Finally, a man who can take a woman somewhere other than the movies.

We walked and walked, talked and talked. I found Frank to be very personable and funny. Frank had a hearty laugh that ended in a high pitched squeal. I loved a man with a good sense of humor. Momma always said, "Find a man that will make you laugh. It's better than a man who'll make you cry." Anyway.

As we walked, a sense of contentment came over me the more I was around Frank. It was uncanny. It was as if time stood still just for us. At one point, I brushed up against him and because I felt so comfortable, I leaned on him and touched his shoulder. I thought, Girl, you don't even know this man, and you're touching him already. I startled myself.

Frank must have thought that I was nuts or horny. But I was drawn to him. I didn't know how quite to explain it. Physically, he was very attractive, well-groomed, tall. But I was drawn more to his calm disposition, his upbeat personality and the tenderness behind his deep brown, soulful eyes. Frank wasn't quick to speak and chose his words very carefully. He didn't talk just to hear himself. Every time I said something, I had his complete attention. I know, because he looked me dead in my eyes. He made me feel like the entire world had vanished and it was just him and me. It was as if we were magnets. The more I fought the attraction, the more it happened. When Frank looked at me, even for a brief moment, the sky lit up and me, too.

Time seemed to escape my tight grasp and made my lips say good-bye to Frank. "Thank you so much for the guided tour and the pleasure of your company," I said.

"You're welcome. I'm sorry you have to leave so fast," he said with a sincere tone.

"Me, too," I said, "But I need to get on the road."

"Speaking of the road. Let me give you exact driving directions. I don't want you to take another detour to Wilmington."

"Oh, you got jokes, huh?" I laughed.

"I just want you to get home safely. Plus, I was hoping I could call you later."

I felt sixteen all over again as I stood in front of Frank and blushed. I swear I didn't want to go. We stood for a brief moment on the steps of the museum in front of our cars. I wanted to lean over and give him a hug, but I refrained. I thought I had been forward enough for one day. So we said our good-byes and went to our respective vehicles. Frank walked me back to my car and said, "Follow me. I'll get you to the main highway. I'll point to your exit and then you get off there. Okay?"

"Okay," I said.

As I followed Frank, I saw him as he looked into his rearview mirror back at me. I was glad, because I had checked him out, too. We got to the highway exit where I was to turn off and he waved and tooted his horn. I tooted back at him as I exited the ramp and waved good-bye.

~~~~~~~~

He was very nice, I thought to myself as I began my three-hour drive home. And all I knew was that I really needed to meet a very nice man. I didn't want to marry him or anything. It was just nice to know that there were true, kind, genuine men still around.

Frank gave perfect driving directions. I got home in record time. I drove to Stephanie's house and picked up Nicole and Jordan. They were so happy to see me and I was so happy to see them. I hurried in the house to gather their things. I didn't want to answer the million questions I knew Stephanie would ask. I was halfway out of the house with the kids in tow when I heard, "Moniqué." It was Stephanie.

"C'mon, Nicole and Jordan. Momma's got to go," I said as I practically dragged both of them as they held hands.

"Moniqué," Stephanie shouted again as she ran behind my car.

I slammed on my brakes and put the car in reverse. I stopped right in front of her. She bent over and gasped. When she stood up, she clutched her chest like *Red Foxx*.

"It's been awhile since you hit the gym, huh?" I said as all three of us laughed at her.

"Girl, I'll talk to you later," Steph said as she walked away, swatting me like a bug.

"Steph, I'll call you later. I promise," I yelled.

"Don't call me, heffa. I don't wanna talk to you now."

I smiled as I drove off. I knew she didn't mean it. And I knew she would be waiting for my call.

~~~~~~~~~

When I got home, there was a stack of junk mail inside my mail slot. I picked it up and threw it on the kitchen cabinet. I figured I would read it later. The kids were hungry, so we ate and watched a movie. Well, they actually watched the movie; I was in a world of my own. My mind was busy with thoughts of Frank and our afternoon together. Like the kids' movie, our afternoon was magical. But I pushed those memories out of my head. I had to. I couldn't allow myself to go there—that place where hope resided. After all, who was I kidding? I was in no mood or frame of mind to deal with another man. I couldn't trust a man who lived in the same city. And especially not a man who lived in an entirely different state. So, it was nice while it lasted.

Exhausted, I put the kids in their own beds and said my prayers. Well, I didn't pray, pray. I said the kids' prayer. "Father, bless me and keep me, from all danger and harm...." Just as I put my leg in the bed, I heard a beep from my machine. I forgot to check it.

*"You have one message. To hear your message, please press one now."* To my surprise, my heart raced. I pressed the button as hard as I could. "Who is it, who is it?" I wondered.

"Hello, Moniqué...this is Frank Thompson. I called to see if you made it home safely. I had a great time this afternoon, and it was wonderful meeting you. I hope to hear from you soon."

"Yes, yes, yes. He called. Okay, calm down, girl. It's just a man. No big deal, right? Now, to be polite, just call him back and let him know you got his message and that's why you're returning his call," I thought.

Frank picked up on the first ring.

"Hi, Frank, this is Moniqué...."

After a few pleasantries, Frank stated, "William told you I

was separated, right?"

"Yeah, he did. And Troi told you I was divorced, right?"

"Yeah, she did. But the reason I'm bringing it up is because I want to get the record straight right off the bat. I don't want you thinking I'm a separated, married man on the rebound."

"Actually, I hadn't thought that at all."

"Good. That's what I'm trying to prevent."

Frank began summing up in about five minutes his current legal status. According to Frank, he had already filed his divorce papers with the court and all they needed was a judge's signature. He was married five years and they had a son. Because of the military, she lived in Georgia, their last duty station, and he lived in Raleigh, his current duty station. He didn't like being separated from his son, but his ex had a job and family there. Frank saw his son, Charles, as often as he could. He and his ex, as a part of the divorce agreement, worked out a visitation schedule that included summer and major holiday visits.

"So, can I ask you a personal question?"

"Well, you're welcome to ask, then I'll let you know if I want to answer it or not," Frank responded.

"What was the biggest issue in your marriage?"

"Trust," Frank said the word before I even finished my question. "She cheated on me," he replied void of emotion, stating the fact only. "If it had been something else, maybe we would have made it, but that wasn't the case. I definitely took it real hard, and rightfully so. The cheating wasn't the only issue, but it was a major one. That is why I always applaud and give props to couples who are able to keep their marriage together. Especially when a major violation occurs. It takes a very, very special man or woman to keep the relationship together. We weren't that

142

special."

"Okay," I said awkwardly. "We can go on to another subject if you'd like." I hoped he wouldn't ask about me and Darren.

"No, I don't have a problem with this one. As long as both of us do the talking."

I held my breath. Frank continued talking, but I was busy trying to come up with a way to explain my marriage without me sounding so nasty and so trifling.

"'Cause I don't know about you, but when I was married, I didn't know Jesus," I heard Frank say as I started to actually listen to him again. "I didn't get saved until after she and I split up. We were separated for two years prior to that. And it was during that separation period that I had to work through some major issues. But as soon as I gave my life to Christ, a huge burden was lifted off me. And you, are you the same person now that you were then?"

"I hope not," I said.

"Then how about we make a deal. From this moment on, your past is your past. And so is mine. Can we just move forward from here?"

"Okay, but can I ask you one more question?" I didn't wait for him to answer me. "Why are you being so open, so personal, already?"

Frank laughed. "I ain't got nothing to hide. Plus, that's just who I am. Now it's up to us to decide where, and if anywhere, we go from here. But I am all about moving forward and enjoying the journey."

And so was I. My tomorrow *had* to look better than my yesterdays, because I had plans, goals to accomplish. I wanted to go back to school for my degree in social work. With the credits

I already had (I quit school after having Nicole), I only had a year-and-a-half more to go.

CHAPTER TWELVE

**M**ommy, mommy. Look at all this mail," Jordan said as he threw the mail in the air. "Boy, give me that," I said as I snatched away the last piece of mail he had in his hands.

The envelope caught my attention. It was a letter from Linda. I recognized her pretty cursive handwriting, so immediately I tore it open and read,

*Dear Moniqué,*

*Greetings in the precious name of our Father and Lord and Savior Jesus Christ. I am writing you this message because lately it seems as though every time I try to talk with you or come see you, something blocks my way. I called you last Thursday, but you were not home, and I was so moved to call you last night, but it was as if something kept me from getting up out of the bed and dialing your number.*

*Nevertheless, I don't know what is going on, but I do know something does not seem right. Don't get me wrong. I'm no prophet, but one thing I do know is that once God knits my heart and spirit with another, I can generally feel or discern when things*

*have gotten off course or out of place. I have sensed a restlessness in my spirit for more than a few weeks now where you are concerned, but I have not been able to put my finger on what it is. Something has affected you; and yes, you appear distant now; and yes, I'm concerned, because I love and care about you.*

*I wasn't going to get any rest until I got this off my shoulders. Last night I was talking to the Lord, and when I began to talk to Him about you, Nicole and Jordan, I began to weep uncontrollably, as if you were being pulled away from God and I was grieving for you. I couldn't fully understand why that was happening to me, and I still don't fully understand it all. But, I do want you to know that I'm always here for you because I am my sister's keeper. God has invested so much in you, Moniqué, it just pains me to watch the enemy with his slick and cunning devices come in and try to steal from you what God has given you.*

*I just have one question for you...How bad do you want it? Whatever it is...I know it's hard when you desire something and you've been waiting a long time for God to move the way you think He ought to move for you. I, too, can identify with that. God's ways, on the other hand, are sometimes different from ours. In God, waiting = suffering. But it humbles us and we benefit from it in the long run, because during the loneliest times of our lives is when we find God.*

*When God is working in your life, He always makes you wait, and during the waiting process, God is preparing you for a miracle, if you just wait on HIM. On CHRIST the solid rock you must stand, because all other ground is sinking sand. Don't sell your birthright to the enemy by getting out of God's Good Graces. DON'T GIVE UP, BUT GET UP. (Read St. John 6:27)*

*Love ya, Linda*

146

I read the letter, not only with my eyes, but with my heart. Tears flowed down my face as I cried from the beginning sentence all the way to the last. Linda wrote me from the depths of her heart and soul. I knew from the start of our friendship that God had created a certain connection between us. But I thought I had ruined it. I stopped talking to Linda just like I had stopped talking to God. I read the letter over and over until I could no longer see the words through my tears.

Jordan and Nicole came over to where I was sitting. They both had on their swimming suits and towels in hand.

"Momma, you okay?" Nicole asked rubbing my back.

"Yeah, Nic, I'm fine. You got your stuff? And Jordan's?" I asked switching gears. I had to be momma then.

"Yeah, Momma, we're ready to go," Nicole answered.

I grabbed my keys, and the kids and I were off to swimming practice.

I talked to Linda a couple of days later and told her simply, "I got your letter. Thank you."

"Moniqué, you know I'm here if you need me," she said reassuringly.

"I know, Linda. Thanks."

~~~~~~~~~

The television evangelist declared, "Once Jesus touches you, you're never quite the same again."

"Amen," I said as I stepped into the shower. The hot water soothed my aching back. I'd had a restless night, floating in and out of dream. The dream seemed to pick up from the last one I had had:

*I saw myself standing before two big boxes. Each box had a pair of arms. The first box was beautifully wrapped in sparkling purple and gold paper, while the other box was wrapped in plain, brown paper. Behind the pretty box were several more, smaller pretty boxes. However, the brown-papered box stood alone.*

*I felt like I had to choose one or the other. And whatever box I chose by embracing the arms, I not only got the big box, but I got whatever was behind the box, too. But right before I made my choice, I woke up.* (Don't you just hate that?)

I didn't know what the dream meant, and I didn't have time to figure it out right now.

"C'mon, ya'll, we're going to be late," I said stepping out of the shower. I rushed and put my clothes on for church.

Nicole and Jordan ran from their bedroom all ready to go.

"Nikki, open the door and tell me how it feels outside." I was trying to decide if I needed a jacket or not.

"Ooh, Momma, you got two flat tires," Nicole said looking at the car.

"Oh my goodness." I ran to the door, putting both of my hands on top of my head. We had forty-five minutes to get across town.

"Go sit down," I told the kids as I rushed to the phone.

Jordan followed Nicole to the couch.

"Can I speak to Darren, please?" I asked the stranger who answered my ex-husband's phone.

"Yo, dis Darren."

"Darren, I need a favor. I have two flat tires and I need a…"

"Moniqué. I'm not AAA."

"Darren. Please. Me and the kids just need a ride to church. I'll fix the tires myself if I have to."

"Why didn't you call any of your peeps?"

148

"I don't know. You're the first person I thought of," I said pacing back and forth.

Nicole and Jordan watched my every move and listened to every word I said to their daddy.

"Ah...right. I'm on my way."

"Hold tight kids. Your daddy is coming to get us."

Darren picked us up just in time to get us to church before the opening song was sung. He fussed the entire time, but I didn't care. I was going to church by any means necessary.

Morning service at First Baptist was jammed packed. The usher seated us in the last few rows of the sanctuary, but even that was okay. I was just glad to be in the house. I really didn't realize how much I missed church until then.

Everyone stood to his or her feet as the officers of the church marched in to the processional. My spirit quickened within me and spoke, "Here we go."

The service began differently from the last time I was there. On that occasion, the praise and worship time was extended as the presence of the Holy Spirit moved throughout the sanctuary. This time the organist played a simple but powerful song. It was one of those songs that if you kept repeating it, it got down into your soul, your inner being. Somehow you felt within you the melodies and chords as they played in your spirit. The combined sounds moved through your nostrils like a sweet, summer morning breeze. All I wanted was to take a deep, soothing, long breath and hold it in. I didn't want to let any of it out. It was food for my soul.

I sat in the chair as if I was the only person in the room and sang to myself, "We worship You, Lord, only You, for it was You who brought us out and You who brought us through...."

As I sang the song, it got so good to me that I had to make it personal. It was my very own personal plea and thanksgiving unto God.

"I worship You, Lord, only You, for it was You who brought me out and You who brought me through…."

The entire congregation sang the song over and over again. I really don't know how long we sang that song, but I do know that every time I sang it, it became a part of me. It rang through my core, and I began to float among the melodies. It was real for me. I thought back to all of the dangers (like driving a hundred miles an hour in bad weather) I had escaped. To all of the heartbreaks (Mark, the abortion) and disappointments (my infidelity to Darren) I had in my life. I thought back to my successes and failures as a woman and as a mother. I saw myself clearly, like never before. The words of the song not only soothed me, but I knew them to be true. I would not have been there if it had not been for God. God drew me back to Him.

I sat in the service dumbfounded and amazed at how good God was to me. How faithful He had been. I didn't have any expectations of the service, but somehow God met an expectation that I had of Him. I wanted, no I needed, to *feel* God again. I needed Him to wrap Himself around me. I needed His total forgiveness and His total acceptance. I had run from God, but now, I wanted to run to Him. And I was just so thankful that when I ran in His direction, He greeted me with open arms.

Suddenly, I knew the meaning of my dreams.

In the first dream when I was at the altar in a church, God was showing me that I had to love God with an attitude of thanksgiving, not for His stuff, i.e. a mate, but to love God for who HE is. And when I prayed, I did get an answer. Just not from

God. God only answers prayers that are in accordance to His divine will. Everything else is praying amiss. And when you pray amiss, the devil answers.

In the second dream, the beautiful box represented Mark. That box appealed to my physical desires but was empty on the inside. There were lots of Marks (the smaller boxes). They looked good, but come on, repeat after me, "Everything that looks good, ain't good for ya." (Amen, somebody.)

God was the brown box, which stood alone, for there is only *one* true and living God. And the blessings that are associated with God are only found "in" God.

And when I love God, truly love Him with my heart, mind, body and soul, I not only get God, but also His stuff (promises, blessings, assurances, security…), too. It's sort of like eating a strawberry without the seeds. Impossible right?

I wept before God as I opened and poured my heart out to Him. I didn't care about the people who sat beside me. There was no time for that. The Spirit of God rained down on me that day like none other. Again, God knew exactly what I needed.

In my spirit, I prayed:

*"Dear God, You know me like no other. You know me better than I know myself, and right now Lord, I need You. I need You to wrap Your loving arms around me and tell me it's going to be okay—that I can trust You with my whole heart and not be disappointed.*

*"Lord, I need You to please forgive me. I'm asking You to forgive me for being selfish and loving You for what You have to give me. I should have loved You for YOU. Like You love me for me. Lord, I got mad and took it out on You. Lord, I am so sorry for hurting and disappointing You.*

*"Lord, I need You to be all that You said You would be to me—my healer, my deliverer, my strong tower. I need Your comfort, Your protection, Your unconditional love. Search me, Lord. Cleanse me, Lord, and renew a right spirit within me. Allow me, Lord, to be all that You would have me to be. I love You."* I ended my prayer.

I know most people have a hard time believing that God speaks, but I heard Him when He spoke to my heart, *"Peace be still, My daughter. I am with you. Trust Me, My daughter. Trust Me with the layers of your heart that have been broken, that have been bruised. The layers that have been stepped on, lied on and cheated on. Trust Me,"* He said.

I heard God's words, and I broke down. The floodgates of my heart erupted and flowed freely, "Lord, I'm so tired of being alone. I'm so tired of being afraid." I had not been alone or afraid on a physical level, but emotionally I was. I emptied myself of all my cares and gave them to the One of whom it is declared, *He cares for me.*

An unexplainable peace came over me. It was as if the Lord, Himself, performed surgery on my heart. After I prayed, painful memories tried to flood my mind. But something about the memories was different this time. I still had them, but they were no longer *painful*.

I knew right then and there that God had placed His seal over my heart, and it read, *"NO weapon that is formed against Moniqué shall ever prosper."*

And I knew *God is not a man that He should lie*. I stood to my feet, a new woman. I was free. Free from my past and free to enter the future. I praised God for all that He had done. I praised Him because He gave me a second chance. I renewed my commitment to live God's way and vowed to serve Him until the day I died.

As for my *love life*...well. On the way home, (Darren came back to get us), I talked to the Lord some more and asked Him, *"Lord, if it's Your will for me to be married, then please, Lord, can You pick him for me? Lord, You know I don't know what I'm doing. Please, Lord, You do it. Not my will, but Your will be done. Lord, don't allow me to go left or right without You. And Lord, when You pick him out, let him love YOU with all of his heart and soul, and can he already be saved? Lord, You told me to be specific in my prayers, and that's what I'm doing. Let him, Lord, love me the way I need to be loved and need me the way I need to be needed. Lord, I want a man, a real man. A man after Your own heart. Let him know whose he is and who he is in You. Let him not be afraid to love, putting his trust in You. Lord, I just want a man who's gonna love me like I'm gonna love him, completely. And Lord, if I can just add one more little thing. Can he have big legs?"* I ended the prayer laughing at myself. Darren and the kids talked the entire drive home.

"What's so funny?" Darren asked as he got out of his car.

"Oh, nothing. Thanks for the ride," I said shutting the door after Jordan.

Darren walked over to my car, shaking his head as he looked closely at the tires. "You know, some bad kids probably did this to your car."

"I figured as much, but what can I do about it now?"

"I'll be back in an hour."

Darren came back in an hour with two brand-new tires. He told me, "I did it for my kids."

## CHAPTER THIRTEEN

The next morning, Monday, I called Shaun at his church.

"Hello. May I speak to Rev. Richardson."

"May I ask who's calling?" said the elderly woman.

"Yes, Moniqué Kennedy."

"Hold on, please."

"Hello, Rev. Richardson speaking," Shaun said in his professional tone of voice.

"Hi."

"Hello?" Shaun pretended like he didn't recognize my voice.

"Shaun. It's me, Moniqué."

"Where have you been? I told my secretary that I didn't know a Moniqué Kennedy."

"Now, you know you need to stop."

"Why? You drop-kick a brother like he stole something, and now you think you can just come back up in here without any grief?"

"Yes."

"Okay, you're right. How you doin' my friend?" Shaun asked as he laughed.

155

"I'm better. Now. A lot has happened since I talked to you, but I'll give you the highlights. I'm no longer seeing Mark and I changed churches."

"What made you do that? I'm talking about church. As far as I'm concerned, you should have dropped that joker, Mark, long time ago," Shaun said, apparently venting his frustrations over my personal life.

"Well, the main reason I changed churches was because of the word being preached. When I was at Mark's church, the preacher was an excellent speaker, but no matter how many words he used, I never remembered anything later. It made me feel good for the moment, but it didn't make me think. This church, First Baptist, makes me think. When he preaches, I feel like he's talking directly to me. I'm encouraged to change, reflect, do better. I like me, now."

"And that has been my prayer for you, you know," Shaun said.

"What prayer?"

"Jeremiah 3:15, *'And I will give you pastors according to My heart, which shall feed you with knowledge and understanding.'* "

"So, what you're saying is that the pastor at First Baptist is giving me what God wants me to have."

"Go on girl, trying to figure things out on your own. First Baptist is a good church. I know the pastor. You'll grow enormously there. But always remember, the power rests with God, not with the man. As a pastor, I share the Word of God and try daily to live for God, but I am not to be confused with God. Your relationship with me, or any pastor, should never be a substitute for a relationship with God. We are only effective when

156

we teach the Word of God with truth, love and power," Shaun said. "Remember that."

"Thanks, Shaun, I'm praying that I do."

"So what can I do for you, young lady? You sound like you want to ask me something." Shaun spoke like a pastor would.

"I need to know where do I go from here?"

"And where is here?"

"I made a decision to live my life for God and to love Him for who He is and not for His stuff," I declared.

"You mean, loving God for a man." Shaun went straight to the real issue.

"Well, that's part of it. I just feel bad being in a relationship with someone based on what they can give me," I said honestly.

"Are you saying that you're in a relationship with God?" Shaun asked.

"Uh...yes. I think so. I want to be."

"Then, Moniqué, you're already where you need to be. Relationship is the key. When you received the free gift of salvation from God, that was only the beginning of your journey, your relationship with Him. And with any relationship, you go through a courting phase."

"You want me to go with God?"

"Yeah. Why not? He goes with you. He goes everywhere you go," Shaun said as he laughed. "But let me get serious. Start by journaling. Write down your thoughts and prayers to God. Be as real and honest as you know how. Allow your heart to speak to you as you write."

"Sounds interesting," I said as he had peeked my curiosity.

"Try it for a week and call me back. I gotta go. Got some pastoring to do of my own."

157

"Thank you, Shaun," I said sincerely.

"Moniqué," Shaun said before he hung up the phone.

"Yes?"

"Welcome back. I've missed you."

~~~~~~~~~

On the way home from work, I stopped by Black Images bookstore. I practically lost my mind with all the stuff they had in there. I walked out with a new journal, three Gospel CDs and a video set of sermons. That night and for the next several days, I wrote in my journal.

*Journal entry:*

I write to You, Lord, because I must. There are so many times in my life when I must write down my thoughts and feelings to You. To the One who's not like any other, who not only understands me, but to the One who made me. To the all-wise and knowing God. I ask and plead with You to search my heart at this very moment. Oh Lord, fix what is broken, mend what is torn, heal what is bruised, close what is open and use what can be used. Make me new. Lord, I come to You because without a shadow of a doubt in my mind, I know that You can do what I can't. I submit to You. Accept me, oh Lord. Forgive me of all my sins, known and not known. Please forgive me. I depend so much on You (although at times it doesn't seem like it) for Your love and guidance. You alone are my rock, my salvation, my security blanket. I can feel Your loving arms around me, comforting me as the sun dawns a new day. Oh Lord, I do thank You. Thank You, for keeping my mind clear, my body strong and my will intact.

You alone are worthy of all honor and praise. I sing praises unto my God, my provider, my source of strength, my fortress amongst my enemies. Oh Lord, I do love You. Honestly, I do. I pray that You never leave me nor forsake me. I pray that the Spirit of the living God dwell deep within my heart and soul. Accept my prayer, oh Lord. I close in the precious and Holy name of Jesus Christ. Amen.

*Journal entry*:

Dear Lord, I pray to You with a heavy heart today. But I also pray to You with a renewed sense that whatever is bothering me, YOU already know about it. Lord, I pray that my faith fail me not and that when I get tired, You give me the strength to stand firm—to stand on Your Word and on Your love for me. Thank You for my new set of mercies. Thank You for protecting me and the kids through the night. Thank You, Lord, for Your constant compassion toward me, Your child. Lord, send a word, speak to me. Open my eyes so I may see. Touch my hands so I may feel You. Oh Lord, I am truly nothing and lost without You. When I write or speak to You, it's like music, flowing freely and without a care. Boundless and unchained. You are to me what air is to my lungs. You love me, for You have proven it over and over again. I am comforted knowing that wherever I am, so are You. Thank You, Lord. Fill me with Your love. Hold me in the palm of Your hand. Rock me in the cradle of Your arms. Oh, how I love You, Lord. This is my prayer, in Jesus's name. Amen.

*Journal entry:*

I will bless You, Lord, in season and out of season. Your praise shall continually be in my mouth. For this is truly the day that

You have made. The angels in heaven rejoice at the sound of Your voice. Oh, praise the Lamb of God, for His truth reigns from everlasting to everlasting. I will not give room for the enemy. I pray right now through the blood of Jesus for inner strength and wisdom. Yes, Lord, create in me a new mind. Lord, Your Word says You have the power to take every thought captive.

For so many of us, we've spent numerous hours and years searching for, and even stealing from others, that special someone just to belong to. To be called "mine" by someone is what we long for. I know, 'cause I went to club after club searching for "Mr. Right," which usually and always turned out to be only "Mr. Tonight." Thank You for keeping me through all of that stuff. As I think back to the lonely nights, drinking stints, partying till dawn because I didn't want to go home alone. As I think of those times, I now realize that I had YOU to go home to. I had YOU to talk to, to go to dinner with and to go to the movies with. I had the best lover the whole time. Lord, I had YOU.

Thank You for never leaving nor forsaking me. I'm so grateful that You took the blinders off and allowed me to see Your marvelous and beautiful light. Oh Lord, praises I give unto Thee. To God be the glory for the things He has done for ME. Lord, I can't speak for anyone else. I can only speak for myself. So Lord, Moniqué Clark says: I love You, Lord. I adore You. I praise Your Holy and Precious name...

This is my prayer in Jesus's name. Amen.

*Journal entry:*

I had to talk to You, Lord. For You alone can hear my words and know my thoughts. I'm fighting just to get through to You. I just don't want to talk to You, but I also want to touch You. I want

You to know that without a shadow of doubt, it is me, oh Lord, standing in the need of prayer. It is me, oh Lord, who needs a touch from the Master. I cry out to You, not in shame, but I cry out to You in the full openness of the Holy Spirit. I'm not ashamed of the gospel of Jesus Christ, and I count it an honor and privilege that I can, at any time or place, go to You in prayer. You alone can help me, this I know...Oh, to be kept. Will You keep me, Lord? I know that I know that You are more than able to do more than I ask or even think. Oh, glory to Your name. King of kings and Lord of lords. I praise Thee, oh Lord, for who You are and not for what You've done. You alone are worthy.

I love You, Lord, oh, I love You. Songs of Your love invade my senses. Melodies of Your grace abide within. Notes of thanksgiving flow freely within my soul. I rejoice, oh Lord, I rejoice. My feet dance to a happy song, my arms wave to Your omnipresent grace, my heart beats to the rhythm of Your love, my eyes behold great beauty and my ears hear Your sweet and gentle voice calling me to Your inner circle, Your inner sanctuary.

*"Come, My child," I hear. "Come and hear the great news I have to tell. Come and hear how I will heal the land and raise up the mistreated. Come and hear how I will let My grace and love abide in, yes, My people. Come, My daughter, to My throne where I will feed you, not grapes of wrath, but bread that will feed your soul and water to quench your thirst. Come all ye that are heavy laden, and I will give you rest. Yes come, yes come to Me. I will not turn you away. I have summoned the mightiest angels to bring you to Me. I commanded all the earth to be still so I could and can commune with you. Yes, My daughter, I have heard you and I see. Don't ever think that I don't see; My eyes are among you all. You are special; you are My beloved; you are blessed, for I have*

*said so. Amen."*

~~~~~~~~

The phone rang.

"Hello?" I said with the pen in my hand.

"Hey, what'cha doin'?" Frank asked.

"Writing in my journal."

"Okay, then I'll call you back later."

"No, it's okay. I'm finished. Hey, you wanna hear something?" I picked up the journal so I could read it to Frank.

"If it's going to make me as excited as you sound, sure. Read on."

I read my last journal entry to Frank.

"Man. It sounded like God took the pen from you and started writing you back."

"I know. I'm sitting here stunned," I agreed with him.

"I get that way, too. When I think about how much God loves me and what He has brought me through, I'm at a loss for words." Frank's voice drifted off.

"Hey, you okay?"

"Got the divorce papers today. It's official," Frank said.

"Is that good news or bad news?" I asked.

"A little bit of both," Frank answered honestly.

*Journal entry:*

Dear God,

This Frank guy has some potential. I'm starting to get that *feeling,* you know. But before I do, Lord, I need to know this is You. Lord, I will not make a move without You. As nice as Frank seems, and frankly, Lord, it's still pretty early, we hardly know each other. But Lord, I don't want to waste one minute more with him if he is not supposed to be in my life. If he is not going to add to my life, don't even let me hear his voice again. Lord, I'm asking You now, remove him, please. When he calls, let me not be home. Let him lose my number—anything, Lord. I'm serious. But if he is, Lord, to be in my life, allow us to really know each other. And give us the courage, really *me* the courage, to date holy, that we may be acceptable in Thy sight. O Lord, my redeemer.

Love You,

Moniqué

## CHAPTER FOURTEEN

I immersed myself in the things of God at First Baptist. The church was a growing and busy congregation with an emphasis on personal growth and development. They had workshop after workshop, and I was eager to learn.

I took as many classes as they offered that also complemented my schedule as a working mother of two, classes like "Character Building." That workshop dealt with issues like being honest with yourself and keeping your word. Then I took a class on "Maturing in Christ." Now, that was a class and a half. We talked about heavy stuff like patience, forgiveness and living holy. And then, I took a class on "Dating in God's Sight." The basic, elementary premise was this, "Date as if God is the third person in the room." Whew, when the instructor said that, it blew my mind.

One of my instructors said that women are the only ones on the planet who will hire someone without a résumé. And then, to make matters worse, we hang on to that person for years, all the while knowing he was never qualified to have the position.

It was because of statements like that that I got the nerve to *interview* Frank. How he did in the interview would determine if we dated or not.

For a solid month, Frank and I talked on the phone every day. Some days we talked longer than others. It just depended on our individual schedules. From the very beginning, Frank was thoughtful and respectful about my life as a single parent. So much so, that he called most days and asked when was a good time for me to talk. And normally, we talked after he had spoken to Charles and I had put the kids to sleep. That way, we had no interruptions on either side—except for the times when he called me right after work. On those occasions, Nicole mostly answered the phone and handed it to me right away. She remarked that I smiled a lot when I talked to Frank.

I must have asked Frank every question discussed in all three of my classes, a few of my own and anything else I could think of. I asked him stuff like, "Why is God important to you? What do you want out of life? Are you looking for a committed relationship or just a booty call? (That was one of the questions I came up with.) Are you capable and willing to love another man's child? Are you in debt up to your neck?" You know, real questions that before attending First Baptist I wouldn't have asked.

I asked Frank so many questions that when we got on the phone Frank would say, "Okay, I'm ready."

"Ready for what?" I'd say.

Then he'd say, "For round one of a thousand questions."

But don't think the questioning was one-sided. I had to answer every question that I asked him, which made our conversations very long most nights. But we had fun with the topics, and we learned a lot about each other in a short period of time.

There were occasions when I would get off the phone with Frank and just talk to God because talking to Frank sort of stirred up something within me that then made me want to talk to God.

166

Now when I talked to God, I wanted to tell Him, "Thank You," whereas when I was with Mark, I went to God to beg for "Forgiveness."

~~~~~~~~

Momma said there were two kinds of men in the world: one who wore slippers and one who wore tennis shoes. For the man who wore the slippers, pull out the recliner, he was there to stay. But the man who wore tennis shoes, he was gone, running!

I wanted to know what kind of shoes Frank wore.

And there was no better way to find out than to talk about sex, or should I say, the lack thereof. So one night, I waited until we had talked about everything else, and just when we were about to hang up the phone, I said, "Frank, I need to talk to you about something."

"Sure, what is it? Sounds serious," he said.

"Yeah, kinda."

"Okay, well, you have my full attention."

"Good, 'cause I need it. Well, you know I'm not too good at sugarcoating anything."

"No, you aren't," Frank said chuckling.

I was grateful for the laughter, because I had gotten a bit serious and scared all at the same time. "Okay, Mr. Jokes. Anyway, like I was saying, basically, I don't want to have sex with anyone except my husband." I paused. "Frank, are you still on the line? Are you still breathing?"

"Yeah, I'm still here," Frank said.

"Are you okay? Can I finish?" I asked because he was so quiet.

"Sure."

"Well, I promised God to have a different kind of relationship this time than all the others. And all my other relationships involved sex, and well, they just didn't work out. I like you a lot, and I'd like to see where this relationship can go with God's help." I held my breath.

"Okay," Frank said, as if what I said was an easy thing to do.

"Have you ever been in a celibate relationship? And are you interested in one now?" My heart stood still, anticipating his response.

"First, is that all you wanted to say?" Frank asked.

"Yes. Do you need me to say anything else?" At that moment, I realized that I never wanted to see him in a pair of tennis shoes. Instead, I wanted his shoe size so I could buy him those slippers.

"No, I don't need you to say anything else. I just wanted to make sure you were finished before I answered your questions. No, I haven't been in a celibate relationship before. But I know I should be in one now because of the relationship I have with God. Moniqué, I like you a lot, too. But first, I want to do what is right in God's sight. Hey, I say we give it our best shot." Frank was an optimist through and through.

There was silence on the phone. Frank let a few more seconds go by before he asked, "Hey, are you still there?"

I had to clear my throat before answering. "Um, um…Yeah, I'm here."

"Why are you so quiet now?" Frank placed the proverbial shoe on my foot.

"I'm shocked at your answer. Pleased, but shocked," I said honestly.

"Why?"

"Come on now, it's not every day that a man, and I do mean, a man, says that he wants to be in a celibate relationship."

"You have a point. But I am trying to be a man after God's own heart and treat you right," Frank said as he further explained his position.

"All right now, suckey-suckey," I said.

"Go 'head girl, you know what I mean," Frank laughed.

"I'm just messing with you. But on the real tip, what about in a couple of months when our feelings for each other start to grow and...?"

"Then I'm going to jump your bones and have my way with you. Nah, nah, just joking." Frank's tone turned serious, "Moniqué, if at any time in our relationship my viewpoint changes, I will let you know."

"Cool, that does it for me."

"Wait a minute. It's your turn. What about you?" Frank asked.

"I feel like you do. If it gets too hard, I promise to talk to you about it."

Jordan walked into the room, rubbing his eyes.

"Momma, can I sleep with you?" he asked climbing onto the bed.

"Boy." Jordan laid right across my legs.

"Hey, Moniqué. Go spend some time with your son. I'll call you tomorrow, okay?"

I hung up the phone and snuggled up against Jordan. He'd be the only male I would be sleeping with for a long time. And that was just fine with me.

CHAPTER FIFTEEN

A few weeks later, I decided to send flowers to Frank. On the card were these words: "Just as flowers bloom, so do friendships."

I wanted to say something nice, but not too forward. Frank called and said he enjoyed the arrangement and that it was a very nice surprise. He said he hadn't received flowers before. But Frank didn't call just to say thank you.

"Would you like some company this weekend?" Frank asked.

"This weekend?" I said, surprised.

"Um, yeah, Moniqué. I was thinking about coming up on Friday."

"This Friday?"

"Moniqué, yeah," he said once again chuckling to himself.

"Sure, I'd like to see you."

"Okay, it's a date. We'll talk about the details later."

~~~~~~~~

It was Friday, a day I was normally off, and I was nervous all day. I hung up on people I was trying to transfer. I couldn't remember people's telephone extensions. And five o'clock quitting time took forever to get there. I hadn't actually seen Frank since our lunch date in North Carolina. Up until that point, I had been relaxed and laid back. No pretenses or games. You know, the real deal. Now that we were going to see each other again, I freaked out.

What should I wear? What should I say? Would he stare at me when I talked and would I have something in my teeth and not know it? These were the questions in my head as I drove the kids to Darren's for his weekend visit.

"Hey, Moniqué," Darren said opening the back door so the kids could get out.

"Hey, Darren," I said, as Jordan bolted toward the house.

"Jordan, get back here and give yo momma a kiss, boy," Darren scolded him for walking away.

"Yeah, how you gonna leave me for a whole weekend and not give me a kiss? You know I can't go to bed at night without one," I said puckering my mouth and leaning my head out of the window.

"Sorry, Momma," Jordan said sticking out his cute set of lips to kiss mine.

"Hey, Momma, if Melanie calls me, can you tell her to call me back on Sunday?" Nicole said before closing the back door.

"Yes, Nicole. I'll tell her," I said looking at her shapely ten-year-old figure just like the little boys across the street were. Pointing to them, I said to my ex, "Hey, Darren. You betta watch those boys."

"Don't worry. I'll keep my eye on them the entire time." Darren gave a rare smile in my direction. I just assumed he was smiling at those boys and not me.

I opened the door to my apartment at the exact moment Frank called to tell me that he was on the road and that he would get into town around nine o'clock. Our date, which he let me plan, wasn't until ten. I played it safe and invited William and Troi to dinner with us. Just in case we had cold feet, we would have them to talk to.

I had to make some big decisions in a short amount of time. Namely, what to wear. Since attending First Baptist, I noticed that my wardrobe had drastically changed. I gave away many of my clothes because I no longer felt comfortable wearing them. They weren't me, and they definitely didn't reflect who I wanted the world, or Frank, to see.

I stood in my closet for a full twenty minutes before picking out a dress to wear. Then I stood in front of the mirror imagining how I would style my hair. Did I want to wear it up or down? I laughed out loud as I thought back to one of my conversations with some new friends at church. We were talking about men, and Sara said, "Honey, God is the only one who looks at the heart. The brothers are looking at your face, hair, nails and feet."

I decided on a simple black dress. Medium length. Nothing too fancy, but it fit the occasion. I felt good in it, and it hid what I needed hidden. I decided to wear my hair down; it looked fuller that way. And I wore open-toed shoes. I had a fresh pedicure, just in case Frank was a feet kind of man.

Frank called around nine-thirty to confirm the directions to my apartment. He was at his parents' home. They happened to live in a neighborhood close to me, a fact that surprised both of us. I actually passed Frank's parents' home each morning on my way to work. Frank was on his way.

The blood in my veins was really pumping. I checked out my

outfit and my face one last time in the full-length mirror hanging on my hallway wall. "Cool," I said while turning in a semicircle. All I thought about was Frank. And the fact that the man I had talked to nonstop for over a month would soon be at my front door.

"Oh no," I said as he knocked. "Who is it?" I asked, not thinking.

"It's Frank."

Duh, I said to myself as I opened the door. "Oh, my," I thought as he took my breath away. Absolutely gorgeous. I put my hand over my mouth slightly to make sure I hadn't salivated. I loved a distinguished looking man. Frank wore a black jacket with a teal green shirt and black pants. He also held the most brilliant, red rose in his hand that I had ever seen. He smiled and handed it to me. His physique paled as his thoughtfulness shined.

"Come in," I said stepping backwards allowing him to come in the door. "Have a seat," I said nervously, walking out of the room leaving him to fend for himself. I don't know what Frank thought, but I just couldn't be in the same room with him. His presence overwhelmed all of my senses. I allowed three minutes to pass, took a deep breath and walked back out to the living room with my coat and said, "Let's go."

Frank politely helped me with my coat and opened the door.

I suggested we take my car because I knew where we were going. Since he had driven three hours to get there, I figured he could use the mental rest, even if it was for only twenty minutes or so.

Georgio's was an Italian restaurant, dimly lit, known for its romantic atmosphere. The food was good, too. Frank caught my attention right away as he held the door open for me as we entered the restaurant. William and Troi were already seated at the table. After exchanging hugs and pleasantries, Frank held my chair as I sat. During the evening, Frank was very attentive and looked right at me when I spoke. He wasn't extremely forward but managed to every now and then place his hand on top of mine. I didn't mind at all; his touch was warm. Frank and William reminisced about their high school days with laughter as Troi kidded me saying, "Girl, ya'll gonna have some pretty kids one day."

"So, what are you laughing at?" Frank said, as he and William turned their attention to us.

"The same thing you are," Troi responded back with a sinister grin on her face.

After talking, laughing and eating for almost two hours, we walked to our cars.

Frank and William shook hands as Troi and I purposefully stood about ten feet away from them.

"So?" Troi began.

"Troi. I'm in no hurry." I could tell by the look in her eye that she had already picked out my wedding gown, cake and china pattern. I gave her a tight hug and joined Frank in the car.

"You ready?" I asked Frank.

Frank covered his mouth as he yawned. "Yeah, I'm ready."

Frank and I got back to my apartment a little after midnight. We walked side by side to my front door.

"See you tomorrow?" Frank asked.

I nodded my head, yes.

"Good night," he said.

"Good night." I went inside and just looked around. For the first time, something seemed to be missing. I fell asleep with a smile on my face.

## CHAPTER SIXTEEN

It was late in the season as Frank and I drove to the beach the next evening. It was a lovely night. The sky was filled with the brightest stars. The ocean was quiet and peaceful. It seemed like an eternity passed before the waves crashed against the shore. There weren't too many people on the beach like Frank and I—a couple. Boy, did that sound funny. Apparently, the interview was over. I was on a date.

Frank was his usual, confident, gorgeous self. He looked like a Calvin Klein underwear model. Sleek, seductive and just all out Fine. I was a little nervous. (What was new, right?) We walked along, barefoot and hand-in-hand as we admired the view. Hotels of all sizes and bustling restaurants lined the boardwalk.

When Frank looked at me, it was just perfect. I mean, the night was just perfect. We were under the many stars God created with His own hands. The wind brushed up against us as the moonlight glistened over the water. The ocean serenaded us and the sand mirrored our footsteps when we walked. Frank stopped and put his arms around me. He asked, "May I kiss you?"

"Yes," I said softly, as I wanted the same.

Correct me if I'm wrong, but when I woke up that morning

and looked at the calendar, it said September. But I swore, at that moment, it sure felt like the fourth of July, because fireworks went off somewhere close by.

The kiss wasn't one of those I-want-your-body-right-now kisses, but it was a kiss just like the night, perfect. The kiss said, "I am attracted to you." It said, "I respect you as a woman." It said, "I admire your strength and your tenacity." "Yeah, yeah, yeah," some might say, "You can't get all of that out of a kiss." Well, yes, I could. 'Cause it was my kiss, and you just have to take my word for it.

That was the only kiss of the evening. That one kiss was complete in and of itself. It was like we knew we needed nothing more. We walked a little bit more as we passed by an arcade room. Frank asked me if I wanted to play some games. I told him, "Oh yeah." After racing to see who could put their shoes on the fastest, we went into the arcade room. I ran to my favorite video game and Frank followed close behind.

"Do you know how to play this?" I said, pointing to the machine.

"Girl, I invented this game," Frank said, pretending to roll up his sleeves.

"Now, I don't want you going home to yo momma telling her that some woman whipped yo butt playing a game."

"I won't tell if you won't tell," Frank said as he placed the electronic card in the machine and pressed the start button. It was a draw. I won two games and so did he. We had so much fun that night.

Frank and I talked and laughed nonstop all the way from the beach to my apartment. Frank turned off the ignition and turned to me and said, "Moniqué, will you go with me?"

I felt twelve years old all over again…like when Micah Smith, my very first boyfriend ever, had just written on a piece of paper those same words to me. Micah even had boxes labeled yes or no, and in fine print, he wrote, check one. (I had my first slow dance with Micah, too. We danced to an R&B classic, *Always and Forever*, by Heatwave.)

"Do people still go together these days?" I asked.

"I don't know what everyone else does, but I'd like to go with you," Frank responded.

"Okay, but I'm curious. Why'd you ask?" I said, with a wide smile.

"Moniqué. I don't want to take anything for granted. I want both of us to have the same understanding as to how we feel about each other and where we stand in this relationship."

"I like that."

"And I like you. My promise to you is that I will be honest with you and do my best to make you happy," Frank said.

Frank walked me to my door, turned around and left. I floated into my apartment, closed and locked the door behind me. I looked around and surveyed all of my stuff. I realized it wasn't *something* that was missing; it was *somebody*. It was Frank.

~~~~~~~~~

Because we had a long-distance relationship, Frank and I actually saw each other two times a month, and we scheduled those times for when the kids were at Darren's. Although Darren and I never really discussed our private lives, we assumed that we both would date responsibly in front of the kids, if at all. And the decision to date with the kids knowing was at our own discretion. Up until meeting Frank, I had decided against it. However, that changed when Frank invited me and the kids to the State Fair.

Nicole and Jordan hadn't met "Mr. Frank" yet, but they had spoken to him several times on the phone when he called the house. Frank suggested that the State Fair would be a good place for them to meet. We would be able to interact in a fun atmosphere as well as get to know each other. I agreed with him, so I asked the kids if they wanted to go and they said yes.

The kids and I went to Raleigh. Frank took us to a beautiful park within walking distance from his place. We walked the trails and fed the ducks along the way. We stopped at a playground and watched the kids run around to the various swings, slides and monkey-bars. Frank played just as hard as Nicole and Jordan did. He was a big kid, just like me. Then we drove to the State Fair. We ate everything in sight. First, we had those large smoked sausages (with everything imaginable on them) and hot dogs. We ate French fries and had fat onion rings loaded with ketchup. We had snow cones and cotton candy. Then, right before we left the fair, we had ice cream.

Nicole and Jordan had their faces painted and rode every ride in the park. Frank and I talked and laughed as we watched them. We even saw the Temptations. (The Temptations jammed, dressed in their red, sequined suits.) The auditorium they sang in was packed full of people. There were no empty seats, so Frank suggested we make a small pallet on the floor. We took off all of our jackets and sat on them. In the middle of the show, Nicole looked at me and asked, "Momma, who are they?"

I said, "They're the Temptations; they're bad, as in good."

"Who are the Temptations?" Jordan also asked.

I looked at Frank, and he looked back at me. We just smiled, and I told them to listen to the music and we would explain who they were later. When we left the fair after several hours, all of us were tired. But we'd had a ball.

When it was bedtime, Frank had already made up his guest room for us. Well, it was actually his son, Charles's, room. That's where he slept when he came to visit his daddy during holidays and the summer. Frank had a big portrait of himself and Charles on the wall.

"Who is that?" Nicole asked me just as Frank came into the room with an extra blanket.

"That's my son, Charles," Frank said, the proud father.

"Where did he come from?" Jordan asked with a child's curiosity.

"He lives with his mother in Georgia. You'll get a chance to meet him during Christmas," Frank said winking at me.

"Christmas? You're thinking that far ahead, are you?"

"Girl, how many times I got say it. I look for...ward."

The kids jumped on the bed excited they would get the chance to meet Charles. Frank and I joined in on the fun.

Frank was a fabulous host. We didn't want for anything. He fed us breakfast, lunch and dinner. And to my surprise, and to the kids' surprise, when Frank cooked, it was actually pretty good. We watched movies and played board games. The kids seemed to enjoy him a lot. They loved to play, and that was right up Frank's alley. Every night, those three wrestled until they were tired. It was fun to see. As it usually was when I was with Frank, our time together went by too fast. The weekend was over and we had to go back to Virginia.

On the way home, the kids didn't question Frank's and my

relationship. I'm not sure if they just didn't care or what. They did say that they liked him. When I got home, Frank had left a message on my machine. He said, "The house is *tooo* quiet. You guys have to come back."

## CHAPTER SEVENTEEN

I thought I told you to call me back in a week?" Shaun huffed after not hearing from me for three months. "You did. I'm sorry, Shaun." I was apologetic.

"That's all you got to say—sorry?" Shaun said.

"Shaun, I have been so busy. You would not believe my schedule now."

"Uh oh, who is he? What's his name?" Shaun asked with concern in his voice.

"Hahaha," I said trying to be sarcastic.

"Haha, nothing. Who is he, Moniqué?"

"How do you know it's a man?" I asked.

"I don't, but I do know that there's something in your voice that's changed."

"Get out of here," I said as I imagined myself as a soft, cuddly teddy bear in Frank's arms.

"No, for real," Shaun said.

"That's just Jesus," I replied.

"Yeah, I will agree, Jesus will do it for you. But something tells me, Jesus got a brother."

I laughed out loud and so did Shaun.

"His name is Frank," I said as I gave in to Shaun.

"And how long have you known him?" Shaun sounded like a big brother.

"A few of months."

"And…." Shaun tried to get the whole story out of me without having to ask a million questions.

"Oh, Shaun. He is so scary," I admitted my inner feelings.

"Scary?" Shaun questioned my word choice to describe my deep emotions.

"Shaun, I want so much for this to be it, but…."

"Have you prayed about him?" Shaun said as he interrupted.

"That's all I do is pray. I refuse to be out of God's will in another relationship."

"Well, that's good. How does this Frank make you feel? Is he good to you?" Shaun asked.

"Oh, yes. I feel like I'm on top of the world when I talk to him, when I'm around him. I feel special, desired, attended to."

"Umm, I'm scared of this Frank, too," Shaun said impressed by someone he hadn't even met.

"Shaun, I could talk about this man forever."

"I see," Shaun replied.

"Shaun," I stopped in mid-sentence on purpose.

"Yes, Moniqué," Shaun said as he seemed to ready himself for my next statement.

"I think I love him." I finally said the words out loud.

"I know, that's why you're scared. But Moniqué, were you scared to love Mark?" Shaun asked.

"Oh, no. I don't know what I was when I was with Mark. But, I know I wasn't scared. In retrospect, I should have been scared, really scared," I said with a smirk in my tone.

"Okay, let's not go back there. Sorry I even brought it up," Shaun said as he paused. "But since I'm there, when's the last time you talked to him?"

I didn't immediately answer Shaun because I had to really think about it. "Umm, when was the last time I talked to Mark?" My mind flashed back to the scene at my car at the hotel in Raleigh. That was the last time. I answered Shaun, "Let's just say it feels like I spoke to him a lifetime ago."

"So, what'cha gonna do about Frank?" Shaun said as he left the dead subject of Mark alone.

"I'm going to keep praying and do what I've been doing— taking it day by day and appreciating every wonderful minute of it, telling God thank You and putting my future in His hands," I said proud of the renewed me.

"You go, girl. Don't wait so long next time to call a brother," Shaun said, ending our conversation.

"I won't. Thanks, Shaun."

~~~~~~~~~~

I *really* liked Frank. I mean, I loved the time I spent talking to him. We had so much fun together, and it wasn't about what we did, but how we did it. Effortlessly. When we interacted, it was so natural and unforced. We seemed to communicate without words. He looked at me, I looked at him, and it was as if a thousand words were spoken through a smile. The relationship was so awesome and scary at the same instance. It was so uncanny when we completed each other's sentences before the other person spoke.

Frank and I were friends. I know most people use that word

so easily without the true meaning behind it. For me, Frank was someone I wanted to talk to about everything. No matter what it was, happy or sad, he was my friend. And I know for a fact I hadn't had that before, with anyone. I would have sex often and early in a relationship, and when you have sex, it clouds things. With sex, common sense gets thrown out of the window. Like when I was with Mark—who in their right mind would rationalize another woman coming to her house at six something in the morning as a parishioner? Point made.

But with Frank, sex wasn't an issue. We knew we weren't going to have it, so we had to concentrate on more important things, like really getting to know each other.

~~~~~~~~

After intercessory prayer one night, I felt a strange sensation in the pit of my stomach. It was gut-wrenching. Have you ever fallen asleep at the wheel and suddenly woke up? That feeling. That's what I'm talking about.

So immediately I got my Bible, went down on my knees and quieted myself before God. I knew whatever that feeling was, it had to do with Frank. I looked toward heaven and cried unto God, "Lord, I'm listening." I had to hear from God, for I knew down in the pit of my being that at that moment I was *in love* with Frank. What I felt for him was more than feelings, it was a knowing. And I wasn't getting confused with desperation, lust or infatuation. I felt that with Mark, but I no longer had those kinds of feelings. It was love—God's kind of love.

But I needed God's approval, first. I wasn't going to act on a feeling or knowing of mine. I had learned from my mistakes, and

I wasn't about to make them again. I knew that my kind of love brought heartache and pain. My kind of love made reasonable, sane people act foolish and turned them into jealous monsters.

So, I prayed and sat before the Lord. I needed an answer from HIM.

Salted tears flowed gently down my face. I didn't even wipe them off. I just sat there on my knees, in the dark. I sat there, unable and unwilling to move. The only light in the room came from the moon. It was so soft and beautiful. A calmness came over me as I felt the presence of God there with me.

Softly, I heard these words down in my spirit. "It's okay. It's okay to love him."

The words went throughout my entire being. They bounced and shouted for joy all through my body. "It's okay," I said out loud. "It's okay." I rejoiced, for I believed what the Lord had spoken unto me. Without a single solitary doubt, I believed. And it felt so good to be in God's will and to be in a relationship that He approved of.

## CHAPTER EIGHTEEN

The kids and I were having dinner at my parents' when Frank called me on my cell. He said he had something important he wanted to ask me. I told him that I could talk to him then, but he was on his way to a meeting and had to talk later.

"Was that Mr. Frank, Momma?"

Both of my parents looked at me at the same time.

"Uh huh," I said to Nicole hoping she would get the hint. She didn't.

"Aw, Momma. I wanted you to tell him I said hello."

"Nicole, will you please eat your food."

"Naw, Nicole. Keep talking. That's the only way we ever find out something about yo momma," replied Daddy.

My momma tapped Daddy on his hand. "Jay."

Daddy replied, "Gwen. So when we gonna meet him?" He turned his attention back to me.

"Only when you need to, Daddy. Only when you need to." I patted his hand reassuringly.

I wasn't ashamed of Frank and me. In fact, I was extremely proud of our relationship. But I just wanted to keep what we had

189

to ourselves.

~~~~~~~~

After leaving my parents, the kids and I went and got some ice cream and then headed home. It was late and they had already stayed up past their bedtime. I stretched across my bed, looking at the ceiling as I waited for Frank's call. He was later than normal. I tried not to worry as my stomach balled into a knot. Just then, the phone rang. I jumped and snatched the phone in one smooth swoop.

"Hey, how are you?" I said as I knew it was Frank.

"I'm fine. How was your day? How're the kids?" Frank asked.

"It was okay, not too bad. And the kids are finally asleep. Nicole told me to tell you hi."

"Make sure you tell her I said hello, too."

"I will. So what's up?" I wanted to skip all the usual conversation and get to the juicy part. "You said you had something you wanted to ask me."

"Nah, I changed my mind," Frank said nonchalantly.

My heart sank like the Titanic. I thought I actually heard screams.

"Oh, okay. Well…," I began to say when Frank interrupted me.

"Moniqué, I'm kidding. I wanted to know if you, Nicole and Jordan would come over and have Thanksgiving dinner at my parents' house. Now, let me warn you, Thanksgiving is like a family reunion at their house, so there will be aunts, uncles and cousins there, too. You know it's only a couple of weeks away."

My spirit rose like the space shuttle. "Sure, we'd love to," I

190

said without a thought to my own plans. I normally had Thanksgiving with my family. How was I going to tell my family that I chose to spend Thanksgiving with Frank? And what in the world was I going to say to Darren? I decided to worry about that later.

"Do you know what time they eat? And do I need to bring something?" I wanted to be prepared well in advance.

"No, but I'll let you know if you need to bring anything. This'll be my first Thanksgiving with my family in about six years, you know."

"And you want to take us over there?" I was surprised and flattered he thought so much of us.

"Moniqué, they have to meet you sometime. Every time I try to get you over there you chicken out and make some kind of excuse. My parents are starting to wonder why I come home so often now."

Frank was correct. He had asked me several times to meet his parents, and I did make excuses as to why I couldn't meet them.

"You come home to see them," I said smiling.

"No, well, yes, but mostly to see you and the kids," he said.

"That's what I love so much about you. You're so open." The words came from my heart.

"Love?" Frank asked.

I knew Frank was attentive, but shoot, he heard everything. My feet were wet, so I jumped in. "Yes, I said love. That's because I do. I love you, Frank." I paused. "And I want you to know that I'm not happy about it one bit," I said like a schoolteacher who had just scolded a student.

"Why aren't you happy about it?" Frank questioned me.

191

"Oh, no, I'm happy. I was kidding about the happy part. I don't think I've ever been this happy in my life. But I am scared."

"Of me?"

"Yes, kinda. Of love, mostly."

"So why are you scared of me?"

"I don't know," I said as I whined.

"Moniqué, you don't have to be scared, especially of me. I'm not going anywhere."

"So, how do you feel?" I asked.

"Are you asking me if I love you back?" Frank said.

"No. Actually, I'm not. I'm secure just loving you for now. But you didn't answer my question."

"I'm feeling pretty darn good right about now. My chest is kind of poking out," he said as he chuckled. "Actually, it's really nice to know where I stand with you and to know that you really care for me. And when I feel the same, you will be the first to know." Frank paused as he gave me a chance to respond.

I didn't, so he continued, "I am not saying that I don't love you and I am not saying that I do. I just don't know right now, and before I tell you that I love you, I want to be sure. I owe it to you and to myself to mean it when I say it."

We left that subject alone and continued our long phone conversation. I was amazed. I told the man that I loved him, and he didn't say it back, and yet, I didn't feel rejected at all. I trusted him, and I truly believed that when he did say it (the "L" word, that is), the words would not only be generated from his mouth, but they'd originate from his total heart and being. And that was worth the wait in spades.

CHAPTER NINETEEN

Thanksgiving was truly a time to be thankful. As planned, Nicole, Jordan and I ate Thanksgiving dinner with Frank and his family. He never lied. There were folks everywhere at his parents' home. His family was a lot like mine, loud. They played cards, dominoes (bones, for the real players), and board games and watched football. Nicole and Jordan fit in well with the other younger cousins who ran around the house. Frank looked just like his daddy, but he had his mother's personality. His mother was soft-spoken but real friendly and attractive. As soon as we walked through the door, Frank made a beeline to his mother.

"Hey, Momma," he said as he reached for her and hugged her tight. "Momma, this is Moniqué."

"Moniqué, it's a pleasure to finally meet you," she said with a smile.

"And, Momma. This is Jordan and Nicole, her children," Frank said as he pulled them from behind me.

"It's nice to meet you two. Can I have a hug?" she asked them.

Before she could even fully open her arms, they had already

embraced her. Frank and I smiled, and I was so glad that Nicole and Jordan were polite.

"It's nice to meet you, too. Can I help you with anything?" I said as I looked inside the kitchen.

"Honey, yes. C'mon in here with me," she said as she grabbed my hand.

I followed behind her as I turned to Frank and stuck out my tongue at him. Frank took Nicole and Jordan and introduced them to the rest of the kids.

"Everybody, this is Moniqué." His mom introduced me to the other women already there.

"Hey, Moniqué," they all said at the same time.

"Hello. So how can I help?" I said as I washed my hands underneath the warm water that flowed from the faucet.

"Oooh, who made this?" Frank's aunt said as she held up a pan.

"I did. It's jambalaya," I said proudly as I recognized my dish.

"Are you Creole?" a cousin asked.

"Naw. I just like to cook spicy food."

Frank stepped into the kitchen, and all eyes turned toward him. "What? Whatever it is, I didn't do it," he said as he pleaded the fifth.

"Frankie got him a woman who can cook," his great aunt said with her hands on her hips and her eyes on my jambalaya.

"Frankie? Did you call him Frankie?" I asked as I pointed in his direction.

Before she could answer me, Frank pulled me out of the kitchen.

With my plate full of greens, ham, potato salad, chittlins and

194

candied yams, we ate. And after dinner, we sat around and laughed as they told old stories about almost everyone in the room. I even told the quarter story about Nicole. Before long, I felt like part of the family. And when it was time to go, I heard his aunt tell him, "Frankie, I think she's the one."

"She *is* the one," Frank said in response.

I pretended like I didn't hear either of them, but I heard them all right.

~~~~~~~~~

On the way home, Frank, the kids and I stopped at a park. The kids saw the slides from the highway and had a fit.

"Mr. Frank, can we stop at the park?" Nicole and Jordan yelled in unison.

"Oh, so ain't nobody gonna ask me?" I said with a playful attitude. I turned around and peeked through the gap between the seats.

"Ma, c'mon, Ma," Jordan said as he batted his big brown eyes at me.

I made arrangements with Darren that he would have the kids for the evening and the next day.

"Okay, but we're not staying long. Okay?" I looked at Frank so he would back me up.

"Yeah, ya'll, we're not staying long," Frank said as he mocked me and winked at them in the rearview mirror.

Nicole and Jordan laughed and winked back at him. Well, Nicole winked; Jordan just closed his eyes.

Frank and I sat on a wooden bench as the kids played on the tall, spiral slide. It was a little brisk outdoors for my taste, so

Frank gave me his jacket and pulled me into him. Without thinking, I blurted out, "Frank, does it bother you when I tell you that I love you?"

"No, because I love you, too," he said. "I knew I loved you a few weeks ago when you told me. But, I didn't want to say it just because you did. I've used these weeks to pray and ask God for His confirmation."

At first, I thought I had lost my hearing, because it sounded like he said those famous three words to me. So, I waited a minute as I tried to act cool, when actually the entire time my legs shook. I just leaned against him, like he hadn't said a word. Frank turned me around and said, "Did you hear what I said? I love you." Frank was serious.

Oh my God, he actually said it. But you know I had to play it cool. I simply replied, "O—kaaay," and left it like that.

We sat on the bench as we watched the kids, hand-in-hand, heart-to-heart, and IN LOVE.

# Plum Crazzzy

## CHAPTER TWENTY

It was Christmas time already. Of course, the kids were excited and racked up on lots of gifts and toys. Between me, Darren and my parents, we went *waaay* overboard with gifts. Daddy, Momma and Darren all showed up at the same time, six a.m. Darren had his Santa costume on and played his Santa routine for the kids. My parents stayed just long enough to see the kids open their presents. It was nice seeing everybody having so much fun. But, Darren didn't stay long, either. Nicole and Jordan had mentioned one too many times that Frank and his son were on their way over. Darren was uncomfortable and it showed.

About an hour or so after Darren left, Frank drove up with company, his son, Charles. Charles was the sweetest little boy. He had a country accent and loved to laugh, just like his daddy did. He was a big hugger, too. From the moment they walked into my apartment for Christmas dinner, we all got along great. I liked to cook and Charles (Big Frank, too), loved to eat. The kids even got along. They didn't fight or fuss. Frank was such a good daddy. He was gentle and had the patience of a kindergarten schoolteacher. We laughed so much that day that I had a laugh headache.

Charles could only stay a week, and before we knew it, it was time for him to go back to Georgia with his mom. Frank asked the kids and me to travel back to Raleigh with him, so we did. We arrived at the airport just in time to get Charles a bite to eat and get him through the extensive security checkpoints so he could make it to the plane. It was the first time I saw sadness in Frank's eyes.

"Hey, man. You know I love you, right?" Frank said as he talked to the top of Charles's head.

Charles reached for his daddy's legs and hid his face.

"You need to always remember that I am proud of you, and I love you," Frank said.

"I know, Daddy," Charles lifted his head and said in reply.

"Make sure you have your mother call me when you get there, okay?" Frank said as he made sure Charles had all his belongings packed away in his carry-on bag. The airline representative motioned to Frank that they were ready for Charles.

"Okay, man, you gotta go. I'll see you again this summer coming up. And, you better be ready for me. I got some fun stuff planned for us."

"Okay," Charles said as he walked away, imagining all the exciting things his daddy had planned for them.

I felt Frank's pain. We waved to Charles as he disappeared down the concourse in order to get to his gate.

Then it was time to go back home. But someone was missing, and we all knew who it was. It was Charles. We no longer felt complete without him. No one ever said the words, but our faces told how we felt on the inside. Frank tried so hard to be upbeat in front of me and the kids. As we made our way to exit the airport, we allowed the kids to run ahead of us (but not out of eyesight). I looked over at Frank, and he had his head down. I gently took his hand and held it in mine. With a gentle squeeze, I tried to empathize with his pain. Without a word, I think he felt my love for him. As I smiled, I tried to let him see that there would be joy in the morning; we just had to make it through the night. And I knew we would.

Frank, the kids and I got back to Virginia around six that evening. Nicole and Jordan went to Stephanie's house for the remainder of the weekend. Frank and I wanted to spend New Year's together. I was home not more than twenty minutes when Frank told me, "Get an overnight bag ready. I'm taking you somewhere."

"Where?" I asked. But he kept our trip a secret. I asked and asked where he planned to take me, but he didn't budge. Nada, not one word.

"It's a surprise, Moniqué. Hurry up and get ready," was all he said.

So I hurried and threw some clothes in a bag. Frank was obviously all ready to go, so we headed out.

The next thing I knew, Frank pulled up to the downtown Marriott hotel. It was an expensive, four-star hotel. The opulent hotel lobby was filled with people everywhere, all dressed up in tuxedos and evening gowns. Everyone looked so debonair. I stood over to the side as Frank checked us in. I heard the clerk tell him, "There will be fireworks on the terrace at midnight."

"Thanks," Frank said as he walked over to me.

Our room was number 1920. We rode and rode and rode the elevator until we finally reached the nineteenth floor. Frank opened the double doors to an elegant and spacious room. I immediately ran to the window to see the view. I knew it would be spectacular, and I was right. We saw the entire city. Christmas lights filled the skyline. All of downtown Norfolk's buildings had their own unique decorations. The cars looked so tiny from the nineteenth floor as they traveled down various streets. It was just beautiful. The night was so clear, so magical. The stars were brighter than ever. And the moonlight silhouetted our faces as we looked out of the window and then back at each other. We could only smile.

Frank and I changed our clothes and went sight-seeing. We walked across the busy street to Waterside, a mall on the city's shoreline. To our surprise, it was packed as well. I lived in the city all of my life and had never imagined going to Waterside for New Year's. (Probably because I liked to stay at home too much. Anyway.) We made our way through the mall as we stopped and ate samples from the chocolate factory, tried on funny hats at the hat shop, and rode the carousel located in the center of the mall. Then we got hungry. Well, maybe not hungry, but we just wanted to eat. Something we both liked to do as often as we could.

Frank and I ate and then headed back to the hotel. Frank looked at his watch and remembered the fireworks were just minutes away. We ran like O.J. back in the day through an airport as we made our way to the top of the terrace. We were met by other hotel guests. They had on their party hats and blew whistles as they laughed out loud.

A few drops of rain fell on us, but that didn't stop the fireworks from going off as planned. It was midnight. The fireworks flew high into the dark sky. They were beautiful, at least the ones that I saw. As everyone shouted, "Happy New Year," Frank stared into my eyes and said, "Moniqué, I love you."

200

He then planted the sweetest and juiciest kiss on me ever. My knees buckled as I melted into his chest. I leaned on him and he wrapped me in his arms as we watched the remainder of the fireworks, but they, by no means, came close to the fireworks I had already seen in my eyes when Frank kissed me. As far as I was concerned, the city could have saved that money.

We had had a long day, so Frank and I headed toward our room. For the first time in our relationship, I wondered if we would sleep in the same bed together. And if we did, would we have sex? We had kept the promise of celibacy up to that point, but hey, let's get real. Honestly, I had gotten a little weary and weak where the subject of celibacy was concerned. After all, I'd never been celibate in any other long-term relationship. I often asked myself why I had to start with Frank. I touched my lips with my finger; I still felt his kiss. I felt sensuous and sexy. I also wanted to feel the heat of Frank against me at that very moment, that very night.

As Frank changed his clothes in the bathroom, I thought to myself, Please, please, man. Don't come out here in nothing sexy, revealing, or enticing. Not tonight. 'Cause I'm telling you, I'm not responsible. I had already pre-repented to God for my thoughts alone. When Frank came out of the bathroom, I didn't even look at him. I just grabbed my bag, walked into the bathroom and quickly closed the door behind me. I smelled Frank's cologne as it lingered in the air. My body tingled all over.

I stood in front of the wide mirror and thought, Now, Miss Thang, what are you going to wear? Nothing, actually crossed my then perverted mind.

"Yeah, Moniqué, wear nothing," a little wicked voice inside my head said.

I shook my head so the voice would go away. I put on my plaid, two-piece pajama set and walked out. Frank greeted me with a grin as he stretched across the width of the king-size bed. It was so soft. He turned on the TV and flipped through the channels. I sat behind him and leaned on his wide back. Frank stopped on one of our favorite shows, *Star Trek*. We were in heaven. We curled up next to each other and watched the show.

*Star Trek* ended up watching us—sleep that is. We woke up the next morning with the TV still on. And so were our clothes.

~~~~~~~~

"Were you as tempted as I was last night?" I freely admitted my struggle and asked Frank.

"If you mean was I tempted to jump on you and rip your clothes off, then yeah, I was tempted," Frank laughed.

"So why didn't you?" I asked. I wanted to hear his answer before I gave mine.

"Ya ain't gonna be mad at me for the rest of your life. I would never hear the end of it; how I messed up our promise to God. And you know it would be all my fault," Frank said.

Frank knew me better than I thought he did.

"Seriously, Moniqué. We did make a promise to God and to ourselves, and I don't want to be the one to mess it up."

Frank and I knew we were obligated to our word, to God. We were aware that the Bible said that God didn't like lukewarm folks. The Bible said He would spit them out of His mouth. And, we didn't want that.

"Yeah, you're right. I would have regretted it."

"I know you would've. But it would have been good, though,"

Frank said with a grin. "At the time, I thought this was a good idea. I wanted us to get away from our normal routine and just relax. I didn't realize how hard it would be for us not to act on our feelings. Let's just keep doing what we used to and not put ourselves in this situation again."

"I so agree," I said as I nodded my head up and down.

I gave Frank a kiss on his cheek and said, "Happy New Year." Then I walked toward the restroom and said, "Oh yeah, a Happy New Year, with ME, that is."

## CHAPTER TWENTY-ONE

Frank stayed in Virginia until Sunday so he could attend church with me. We wanted to be in church together on the first Sunday of the new year. I surprised Frank and took him to Shaun's church. It would be a surprise for Shaun, too. I had promised Shaun several times I'd visit but never got around to doing so.

Frank and I sat about four rows from the front of the sanctuary. I liked being up front. Anyway. The atmosphere was electrifying. And the praise and worship was off the hook. We felt the presence of God in that place. It was unmistakable.

Shaun didn't sound like I imagined him to sound in front of his congregation. The person I heard that morning was serious and authoritative in his tone. And yet, at the same time, he was gentle as he spoke about a gentle God. There, Shaun was Reverend Richardson!

And Shaun, did he preach? Oh, yeah, he preached. As he rose from his seat and stood at the pulpit, Rev. Richardson said, "Turn with me in your Bibles to Genesis. We will begin with chapter thirty-seven."

Frank handed me my Bible that he was holding on his lap

and then opened his. We stood along with the rest of the congregation for the reading of the Word. Shaun read.

"You may be seated in the presence of God," Rev. Richardson instructed.

We all sat down in unison. I looked at Frank as if to say, "Get ready." Frank read my thoughts and said, "I am."

Frank and I turned our attention to the pulpit where Shaun stood confidently. He spoke for about forty-five minutes. He was on a roll.

*"If you are faithful to God through your pit days, prison days, when you were rolled over and stomped on, God will bless you so good, He'll make you forget all of your toil."*

"I know that's right," I said aloud in agreement with his words. I heard others in the congregation say, "Amen."

*"God will cause you to be fruitful in the land of your affliction. For everywhere Joseph went, you see these words... 'And the Lord was with him.' It does not matter where you go and it does not matter who you are...It's about who you have WITH YOU."*

Frank and I reached for each other's hand at the same time.

*"When it is God's time in your life for you to pass that midnight of your life, when you are finished going through, finished enduring, finished holding up your hands, finished hanging in there...Oooh, the break of day begins to appear. The devil can't stop it; your enemies can't stop it; you can't stop it,"* Rev. Richardson declared.

The congregation rose to their feet along with Frank and I. I waved my hand to Shaun as I told him, "Boy, you better preach, preacha."

*"When the sun gets ready to shine, when God gets ready to bless you, when God gets ready to deliver you, when God gets*

*ready to be your help and your strength...You'll say like Job said: He knows the way that I take; it wasn't a good way; it was a hurting way; it was a crying way; it was a painful way...."*

Frank pulled out a piece of paper and pen from his Bible and wrote something down. He put the paper and pen back in his Bible.

*"But HE knows the way that I take, and when He's tried me, Job said, I'm coming out; I'm coming out as pure gold; I'm coming out with a new dance; I'm coming out with a new testimony; I'm coming out with a new joy; I'm coming out with a new outlook on life; I'm coming out with a new praise; I'm coming out with a new victory."*

Tears rolled down my face as I remembered God and His faithfulness to me, how He had honored my prayers and given me so many chances to do right. My heart flowed with gratitude to God.

*"Because, weeping may endure for a night, but joy is coming in the morning, and I have come to tell you...it's morning time. God's getting ready to shine on somebody, to shine in somebody, to shine through somebody."* Shaun sweated profusely as he conveyed the Word with power and conviction.

Frank stood to his feet, nodded his head and said, "Amen. Amen."

*"Hold on. You're on the verge of your miracle. You're getting ready to get a breakthrough. God's getting ready to deliver you, to see you through, to bring you out, to give you the victory. God's getting ready to give you those things that the enemy took from you. This is your year, your day, your month. God's getting ready to bring you OUT...,"* Shaun declared as he stepped down from the pulpit. He paced the red-carpeted aisle as he held the

microphone in his hand. Rev. Richardson patted congregants on their shoulders as he said, "You, you, God's talking to you."

He took a few more steps and said, "I'm talking to you. God's going to bring you out."

Then he pointed to me and Frank and said, "You two, God has great plans for you. Hold on to His hand, don't ever let go."

Rev. Richardson continued to minister to his congregation as all stood to their feet. Tears flowed freely. Hands were raised everywhere. People shouted, "Hallelujah" and "Thank You, Jesus."

I heard Frank say, "Glory to Your name, Jesus. You are so worthy of all the praise."

I lost it after that. I had to get my own praise on. And that's what I did. I shouted up and down the aisle.

Shaun's sermon was just so powerful. My spirit was uplifted and encouraged at the same time. I needed to hear that word and God knew it. Frank looked at me and I looked at him. At the same time, we both said, "This is going to be a good year."

We both felt that something was going to break loose in our lives. It was one of those "I know that I know that I know" feelings. Only a true believer would understand. When you know, you just know. Frank and I didn't know the what or the where, but we knew the why. It was because God promised, Jesus said it, and because we were His children, we were assured the victory. Not sometimes, but at all times. The message was incredible.

As Frank and I walked to his car, I looked over at him and said, "I need to go to Darren's. I need to get things right between us." I had noticed, since I began dating Frank, that Darren had slowly begun to distance himself even more.

Frank stopped and held my hand, "Then go get it."

## CHAPTER TWENTY-TWO

My stomach was in knots as I knocked on Darren's door. I hated coming over without calling first, but I felt I didn't have a choice this time. Darren's neighborhood was shockingly quiet for that time of the day. As I stood on his step, I could even hear some birds chirping. With my head lowered, I tapped my foot nervously on the concrete pavement. A few seconds passed when I heard, "You want something?" Darren said through the screened door.

"Darren, I need to talk to you about something important," I said, and I reached for the handle on the door to open it. The door opened slightly, but Darren pulled it back to close it. I stepped back two steps and took a deep breath. This is harder than I thought it would be, Lord, I prayed in my thoughts. I heard God say, "But you can do it. Just open your mouth, and I will fill it with words." So, I tried again. "Darren, please, can I come in?" my tone whined.

Darren swung the door open and walked away.

I stepped slowly through the front door and stood in the doorway. I wasn't going to move unless he told me I could. He sat at the grey card table.

"You can sit down," Darren said as he lit a cigarette.

"When did you start smoking?" I asked without thinking. I walked and sat on his loveseat.

"When did you start to care?" Darren retorted.

Lord, I thought, You said You were going to help me here. That time, I whined to God.

"Darren, I have always cared about you, and before you say something, please hear me out first. Please."

Darren's body language was tense as he inhaled deeply on his cigarette. I took his no response as an okay for me to keep talking.

"There's no easy way to say this but to say it, so, here it goes." I inhaled, too, but with air into my lungs. I wanted to say what I had to say in one breath. "Darren, I should have said this a long time ago, and I didn't. But I want you to know right now that I am so sorry I ruined what we had. I'm sorry I cheated on you. It was wrong, and I was wrong. And today, I'm asking… no, I need, your forgiveness. I'm trying to change and I need…"

Darren lifted his hand like he didn't want to hear anymore. He sat up in his chair and squashed his cigarette in the palm of his hand.

I held my breath. I was scared.

Father God, please allow his heart to heal, right here, right now. Allow both of us to move forward in grace. I prayed in thought only.

Darren stood up.

I prayed some more, Okay, God. What's up, You see me, don't cha?

Darren walked over to the loveseat and stood right in front of me.

I closed my eyes and prayed, Lord!

"Moniqué, you're good peoples. You always have been. But it's going to take me more time than you to get over what happened."

My shoulders slumped over.

"But I will say this, I'm willing to try."

I opened my eyes to see Darren's strong black hands extended out to me. I placed my hands into his and he lifted me up. Darren and I hugged each other tight. It was the first time we had touched each other in years.

In my spirit I heard, "Love covers a multitude of sins."

## CHAPTER TWENTY-THREE

I slammed the door to Ms. Leslie's office as hard as I could. Her secretary tried to stop me, but I pushed her out of the way. Ms. Leslie was startled.

"What is this?" I said, crazily waving a yellow envelope in her face. "I got this in the mail over the weekend," I yelled.

Ms. Leslie didn't even ask to see it, she already knew what it was. She stood to her feet and walked around her desk. "Moniqué, first, calm down and let's have a seat." She pointed to the chair.

"Calm down. You want me to calm down!" were the only words that came out of my mouth.

Ms. Leslie reached for my sleeve. I yanked my hand away.

"Don't you touch me." I stared at her.

She walked back around her desk and placed her hand on the phone.

"Oh, you don't need to call security," I said looking at her hand.

"Good, I'd hate to have to do that. But you seem to not want to give me a choice in the matter," Ms. Leslie said as she mouthed to her secretary through the glass window, "I'm okay."

My head turned toward the window and then back, like the

girl in the Exorcist.

"You trying to fire me. I can't believe this," I said with my voice raised.

"Moniqué, you have had more than enough time to get better, and it seems...."

I interrupted her. "What is 'more than enough'? Especially since the strenuous working conditions here caused the injury to begin with."

The tension was thick in that room.

"Moniqué, you either take this new position or you choose to be terminated," she said as she avoided eye contact.

"That simple, huh?" I asked as my eyes glossed over with tears.

"I'm sure for a person in your position...." She stopped, switched her statement and said, "No, your decision is not a simple one."

I wiped my eyes refusing to allow her to see a tear fall in her presence.

"You got that right. You know if I take this position you're offering, I'll do more damage to my hands?" I wanted her to know the magnitude of the situation.

"I will need your decision by the morning." She moved her hand from the phone and looked away.

I sat down. Reality set in very quickly. "I need to take the rest of the day off. Is that okay?" I said taking a quick pause between each word.

"Sure."

"Actually, I'll need the next two days off," I said.

"That's fine. However, I will need to see you first thing when you do come in. Do you understand?"

214

"Better than you think," I replied.

With every ounce of dignity I could muster, I raised myself from the seat and looked her in the eyes. "I'll let you know what my decision is in two days," I said opening her door.

The secretary almost fell on her face. As she entered Ms. Leslie's office, I heard her saying, "Girl, I thought she was going to whip yo a...."

I turned the corner just as the secretary's voice faded out. Everything after that point was hazy. I don't know how I got home. And I didn't know how I was going to live.

~~~~~~~~

"Hey, is everything okay? I called you at work and they said that you had left for the day. Are you feeling all right?" Frank was concerned.

"I'm okay. Just a little tired. Can I call you later?" I sounded like I had the flu. I didn't want to burst into tears, so I remained quiet about the job situation.

"You sure you okay? Can I help you with anything?" Frank insisted.

"Naw, dear. You can't help me with this. I wish you could. But you can't." I knew Frank meant well, but he was only a man. I needed God.

"What is it? Try me. You never know, I might surprise you."

"They're trying to fire me at work. Either I take a position I know will cause me more harm than good, or I have to quit. Simple as that." I was frustrated.

Frank was silent for a moment and then said, "Monique. Whatever happens, I'm here for you. It'll be okay." He tried his best to reassure me. He paused again and said, "Shoot. Quit."

Frank's words hung in the air. I saw them clearly spelled out.

"Did you hear me?" he said. Frank, the guy I loved, said, quit. He said, QUIT.

I almost dropped the phone. I got such an attitude with him. Immediately, I questioned if he really cared about me. Was he playing some kind of game on me? As I heard his words over and over again in my head, I got mad. I was so angry.

"Frank. I gotta go. I'll talk to you tomorrow," I said as I hung up the phone and unplugged the cord from the wall.

I thought aloud as I paced my bedroom, "This man has *got* to be tripping. How is he going to tell somebody to quit a job, just like that? He knows all the stuff I got to do. How am I going to quit! Then he got the nerve, the audacity, the gull to say, 'It's going to be okay, I'm here for you.' Yeah, right." I pretended Frank was in the room and asked him, "Do you know how many times I have had a man tell me those exact words? What makes you any different?"

That night, before I went to bed, I checked in on the kids. Nicole lay on the top bunk alone. She looked so peaceful. I bent down to check on Jordan, who slept on the bottom, when Nicole called my name.

"Momma?"

"Yes, Nicole."

"Good night, Momma, I love you."

"How much do you love me?" I asked.

"All the way to Pluto," she said as she pointed her finger to the sky. Nicole had said those same words to me since she was three years old. It was our special game between the two of us.

"That's a lot of love, Nicole, a lot of love," I said climbing the steps of the bunk bed. I wanted to look into her eyes.

"Momma, you say that all the time," Nicole said as she extended her arms to me and hugged me around my neck.

Closing my eyes I prayed, "Lord, I can't let her down, ever." I told Nicole, "Go to sleep, little girl. You have school in the morning." I immediately thought about her future college tuition. How was her college fund going to grow without a job?

Nicole rolled over to her usual spot on the edge of the bed. I was glad the top bunk had rails. I climbed down the steps and headed for the door when I heard, "Mommy?"

"Yes, Jordan." I knelt down beside his bed. I thought he was sleep.

"Can you help me talk to God?"

"Why do you need help? You know how to talk to God," I assured him.

"I don't know."

My mothering experience told me that Jordan wanted some quality time like I had just given Nicole. "Sure, Jordan, c'mon let's pray," I said as Jordan got on his knees beside me. "Do you want me to start or are you going to start?" I asked him.

"You do it," Jordan said nudging me.

"Give me your hand and let's pray. Father, we just want to say thank You for another day. Thank You for Your love and for being good to us. Thank You for Your Son, Jesus, and bless everybody we know, Amen." I opened my eyes.

"And God, please, bless my momma. I love her a lot," Jordan added as he got off his knees and gave me a big hug.

I hugged him back as tight as I could without breaking a bone. A part of me didn't want to let go. I needed a hug, too. I kissed him on his tiny lips and threw him in the bed. He liked

217

being thrown. I heard Jordan giggling as I turned off their bedroom light and closed the door slightly. I knew I wasn't going to bed anytime soon and didn't want the light from my room to keep them both awake.

My kids were the pride and joy of my life. So many times I wanted to throw in the towel and just quit, but I couldn't. I had them, and I knew they needed me. Their love for me was so unconditional. Tears welled up in my eyes. My heart was heavy. I wanted to be optimistic, but everything looked so bleak. I didn't want to be a statistic. Society already looked down on single-parent homes—said we didn't love our children, said we were too busy doing our own thing to take care of them. Society said that our lifestyles were erratic and careless. They painted a picture of our kids at school in raggedy clothes, misbehaving, and labeled them ADHD. You name it, they placed the blame on single-parent homes, and I was sick of it.

So I kneeled down by my bed and prayed, "God, You know my situation. Lord, You've been there every step of the way. And I thank You for sustaining me and keeping me this far. When things got rough and I wanted to quit, You gave me the strength to hang in there just a little while longer. Lord, You promised me that I would be the head and not the tail. Lord, right now, I claim victory in this situation." I grabbed the pillow and muffled my cry. "Lord, I don't believe it is Your will for me to be unemployed and out on the streets with two children." (At least I hoped that was not God's will for my life.) I quieted myself so I could hear from the Holy Spirit.

Then I heard, "You have ONE option."

Oh my God, I was shocked. I really didn't expect Him to answer me that quick.

I said aloud, "One option?"

"Trust Me," He said.

A light bulb turned on for me. I had an epiphany. God was taking me to another level of trust.

I hadn't made a decision one way or the other about the job, but I trusted God and had faith enough that God would work things out for my good. I believed the Bible when it said, "God neither slumbers or sleeps." So if God was going to be up all night, why should I? I went to bed.

## CHAPTER TWENTY-FOUR

I'm not going to lie; I was jittery all that day. I wasn't nervous when I initially woke up, but as the day wore on, I was. In my mind, I went over my options. I thought, I'll just use up all of my leave time. No, I'll just quit and take my chances. No, no, that's taking the easy way out. Shoot, let them fire me. Then I'll just sue the pants off them. No, that's vindictive and mean.

I went back and forth. I got so emotionally tired that I decided to take a nap. So I laid down. I moved to the left, then to the right. I laid on my back, my side and then my stomach. Nothing felt right. I laid in the bed and just looked at the ceiling, then the clock, then the door, then the…you get the picture.

Then the suggestion, "Look in the envelope," came to mind.

I shrugged it off. I didn't feel like looking at it. Call it denial, call it what you want, but I wasn't going to read that mess. I tossed and turned, tossed and turned. I couldn't get any sleep to save my life. The suggestion got even stronger than before. I gave in. "What the heck," I said, "I can't sleep anyway." I got up, sluggish and with half an attitude, and pulled out the envelope I had stuffed into my dresser drawer. It was so thick. I didn't know where to start. I shuffled through the stack and a couple of pieces of paper dropped on the floor. Great, I thought.

Picking them up, it was as if lightning struck. I read one piece of paper in particular. It was the summary page that detailed how much money I'd receive if I quit on or before the first ninety days of the year. It was *a lot of money*. My pulse raced as I jumped up and reached for my purse. Rummaging through all of the paper, candy and pens, I found my calendar. Upon opening it, I realized that the ninetieth day was March thirtieth. I studied the date. Then it hit me. I was in that ninety-day window! I was about to get PAID.

Deep in my spirit, I heard, "Quit."

I called Frank. I had hoped he would talk some sense into my head. But I first had to apologize for practically hanging up on him. I knew he had tried to call, but I had the phone unplugged.

"Frank, I am so sorry, please forgive me, I had a lot…"

Frank interrupted me before I continued, "Moniqué. You're fine. I know you're under some stress. Just talk to me. Tell me what's going on and how I can help."

I painted the bleakest picture I could for Frank as I saw it then. He asked me one further question, "Now, you told me what the job said, now tell me what God said about the job?"

So I told him. And do you know what Frank said? He said what he said yesterday, "Then everything is going to be okay. I am here for you. Quit."

Great! Just great. He was supposed to talk me out of it, and he didn't. What would happen if God meant something else? What if I didn't really understand?

"Quit," I repeated Frank's response as I got another attitude with him.

Easy for him to say. He's got a job. Yeah, he'll be by my side and got my back, huh? I had men tell me that who I had been with for years, but they didn't mean it. Why in the world should I believe him? I didn't say any of that to Frank 'cause I was immediately convicted within my spirit. I knew the answer to my own question. I should have believed him because he had never given me a reason not to. He had proven over and over that he was not like anyone I had ever dated. Frank stood alone. He was not to be compared to anyone in my life. But maybe God. Frank seemed to love me unconditionally, just like He did.

I had to admit, though, there was *something* in Frank's voice—in his tone and in his words that calmed me and soothed me. For in the pit of my being, I knew and even understood, that everything would indeed be okay. So, I told Frank, "I'm going to do it. I'm going to quit my job."

I knew in the back of my mind that I'd keep it a secret, especially from my family. There was no way I could explain it to them. They would have thought I had lost my ever-loving mind.

## CHAPTER TWENTY-FIVE

The ninetieth day of the year. Shaun had said that God had great plans for me and for me to hold on to God's hand. Well, I decided to hold on to God with both hands.

Frank had called already. I suppose he wanted to reassure me. He probably really called to make sure I hadn't changed my mind. I hadn't, but my flesh sure acted fleshly. My mouth praised God, but my insides cried, "Are You sure, Lord? Are you sure this is what You want me do? Do You realize what You are asking of me? This is a big step, Lord." I paused between each question as I allowed God the chance to answer me.

I went on and on as I talked to the Lord, but then I looked at the clock. It was time for me to go to work. So I asked the Lord, "Okay, Lord, can you give me a sign? A confirmation?"

I'm not sure if I was looking for lightning to shoot out from the moon or what, but I needed a sho 'nuff sign from the Lawd. I tried calming my nerves by picking up my daily word for the day. Usually I read the article first then the quote they had to go along with it, but not this time. I went straight to the quote. I asked for a sign, and boy did I get one. The quote was, *"Why put a question mark where God has already placed a period?"*

Oh my God. Was that plain or what? What confirmation from the Master. With all the power that was in me, I got up off that bed with a quickness, grabbed my purse and keys and headed out the door with a purpose. Oh, yes, I had somewhere to go. I went to quit.

And I did just that. I walked into Ms. Leslie's office with a grin and left with a broad smile. Not to mention a fat paycheck. I signed every piece of paper she needed me to sign.

A serene peace was all over me. I mean, complete peace. Philippians 4:7 says, *"And the peace of God, which passeth all understanding, shall keep your heart and mind through Christ Jesus."* And God was so good that He gave me an extra ounce of joy to boot. Hallelujah.

On my way out, I phoned Linda. I couldn't make it up to her desk to say good-bye personally. She answered her phone with her usual happy self.

"Linda, I'm leaving,"

"Okay."

"No, Linda, I mean, I'm *leaving*," I said trying to convey the enormity of my statement.

"Okay, see you later," Linda said, like it was no big deal.

There I was, a single parent with two children, a car and an apartment, etc., quitting my job. And all she had to say was, "Okay." I had a temporary moment of weakness.

I thought she was my friend, was my first thought.

I had to admit, I sort of had a little attitude with Miss Linda. Of all the people I knew, she had to understand what I was going through. And all she had to say was, "Okay." Then the Lord quickened in my spirit and said, "See, she trusts Me, too."

I quickly repented and started to praise God as I walked to my car. I sat in my seat and pushed in my old *Sounds of Blackness* CD. Contemplating what I wanted to do with the rest of my day (as well as the rest of my life), a song played. I heard, "I don't know what today is offering, but I'm not worried about anything, 'cause I know who holds the future."

Another sign from the Lord saying, "Trust Me."

I pulled out of the parking for the last time and said to the Lord, "I do, Lord. I trust You."

## CHAPTER TWENTY-SIX

I knew I couldn't explain what I did almost a month ago to most people. Actually, there were times I called myself crazy. Who in the world, in their right mind, quits a job and doesn't look for another? Who quits a job when they're the sole bread winner in the family? Instead of job hunting and résumé dropping, who goes jogging? When I should have been worried and stressed out, who was home relaxed, reading a book? When I should have saved every dime I had left, who went to lunch and to a movie?

It was me! I was crazy enough to believe that God would do what He said He would do. And I refused to depend on one soul for any of my needs. God said in His Word that I should *"take no thought for tomorrow."* So I didn't. God told me that He had *"never seen the righteous forsaken nor His seed begging for bread."* So I believed I would have food. God said that *"He would supply all of my needs according to His riches in glory."* So I didn't worry about how I was going to get this and how the kids would get that.

I never, ever asked for a helping hand. And, I didn't ask Darren for more child support. I didn't even file for unemployment. I kept my entire family out of the loop for weeks. I messed up one day, though, when I got bored and went over to my momma's house. Then and only then did I tell her the truth. You should have seen the look on her face when I told her, "God told me to quit." I knew for sho she was going to call the mental ward people on me and take my kids.

Instead, I walked by faith and not by sight. And I enrolled in school. I was going to get my degree! I refused to be moved by what it looked like. I promise, I had more good days than I had bad. I praised God for breakfast, lunch and dinner. I had a praise on my tongue continually. I'd walk up and down my hallway and shout to the top of my lungs, "Glory, Hallelujah. I thank You, Father." I learned to depend on Him and only Him to take care of me. He said I was His child. So it was His responsibility, His duty to do so. But I found out also, it was His great pleasure to take care of me. In fact, God had been waiting on me to allow Him to do just that. He had been waiting for me to give Him free reign in my life. God had waited patiently for me to say, "Not my will, Lord, but Your will be done."

With my severance pay, I tithed regularly and increased my offerings. I paid all my bills off, except my car note. And that, I paid months in advance. When I wrote a check, I'd say to God, "You go, God. Make a way for me." When my child support payments got delayed, miraculously I'd go to the mailbox and receive refund checks from off-the-wall accounts I had years prior. The electric company said I had a previous credit on my account, and so I didn't have to pay any electric bills. I'd go grocery shopping and all of a sudden, that day was double coupon day. Or everything I needed was on sale. I had more money unemployed than when I worked. And when I filled out the forms for financial aid to go back to school, I got a full scholarship, including tuition and books!

Nicole and Jordan were happier than I had seen in a long time. They enjoyed it when I took them to school and picked them up. Oh, you should have seen their faces when I went on their field trips. I don't know who smiled more, me or them. I must have taken three million pictures. They introduced me to all of their classmates. Oh, it was incredible.

And Frank. He was there the whole time. He didn't push. But I know he prayed. I felt his prayers, along with Linda's and Shaun's. They kept me encouraged and steadfast. They fed and reminded me of God's Word and kept me lifted up before Him. But they also left me alone. They knew that I had to do some things alone. I was like a baby bird. I had to learn how to fly on my own. And I did.

"Why should I creep when, within my soul, I know I can soar?"

~~~~~~~~

*My morning journal entry:*

Oh, Holy and Precious Jesus. I greet You with a sincere and grateful heart. I am so full of words, I don't know where to start. You have allowed me to be free within myself. For the first time, I am solely relying on YOU, Your mercy and Your grace. Like Simon, You told him to go out into the deep waters for that's where his blessings were. Well, that's how I feel, like I'm in deep water, with no ship, no boat, no life raft or lifejacket, but I'm floating on Your love and grace. I'm not sinking, for You hold me in the palm of Your hand. Oh Lord, how I worship and praise

You. My heart is overjoyed with just the mere thought of Your majesty. You, who sit high and look low. You, who in spite of my faults and shortcomings, chose to look past all of that and saw my needs. You asked, "Do you want to be made whole?" You didn't allow me to wallow in self-pity, but You picked me up with Your finger of love and rocked me in the cradle of Your loving arms. Oh, precious is Your name. How worthy You are to be praised. I adore You, Lord. I love You, Lord, I really do. Accept my prayer in Jesus's name. Amen!

## CHAPTER TWENTY-SEVEN

The anointing had been in the Hampton Convocation Center all week long. The building was located right on the campus of Hampton University. I hoped one day to send Nicole there. I was so excited about the revival Stephanie and I had attended together. And I was excited that Frank was finally able to join me. Each night I had to fill him in on the service after I got home. That night, he would be able to see for himself what I had seen all week.

As Frank and I drove to Momma's house (so she could baby-sit), Nicole and Jordan sang, "Momma's got a boyfriend, Momma's got a boyfriend, and his name is Mr. Frank, and his name is Mr. Frank."

I arrived at Momma's with a wide smile on my face as Frank turned around in his seat and tickled them before they got out.

"Hey, Momma," both Frank and I said as we walked in the den.

"Hey, kids. Big ones and small ones," she said as she worked on her crossword puzzle. She didn't even look up.

"Ma, the kids went upstairs. We gotta go, okay?" I said as we turned right back around and walked out of the door.

233

"Hey, Moniqué. Stephanie said she'll meet you at the Convocation Center and to save her a seat," Momma yelled out the door as Frank and I got into the car.

~~~~~~~~

The Convocation Center was a huge, dome-like building. It maybe sat about ten thousand people. The building had large, clear windows with sort of a brownish tint to them. Inside the auditorium area, the ceiling seemed to hold a million lights. There were rows upon rows of portable seats in the center area. The stage was moderately decorated with shrubbery. A piano was to the left, and in the center of the stage was the podium.

I grabbed Frank by the hand and told him, "Follow me, I'm going to try and sit where me and Stephanie sat last time."

Frank followed me as he looked around at all the people who had arrived. I walked and walked, but I couldn't remember where Steph and I sat.

"Are you sure you know where we're going?" Frank kidded me as he poked me in the back.

Just then, I heard, "Moniqué!"

Frank and I looked up in the direction of the yelp.

"Stephanie!" I said as I saw her jump up and down in the narrow aisle.

"There she is," I said as I yanked Frank's arm to follow me. I climbed the stairs and reached her. "What are you doing here? Momma told me to save a seat for you."

"Girl, I couldn't wait on your slow butt. I'm too excited. Hey, Frank," Steph said as she dismissed me and turned her attention to Frank.

234

Frank gently slid me to the side and reached for Stephanie. They hugged.

"Good thing you got here early. We probably wouldn't have had a seat," I said to her as I looked at all the filled seats.

"Girl, I know. But I figured tonight would be off the chain and a whole lot of people would come since it's the last night," Stephanie said.

"Yeah, I guess you're right."

"Frank," Stephanie said as she talked across me. "Man, you missed it. This brother has been on fire all week long. And your girl, did she tell you her word God gave her?"

I poked Stephanie with my elbow and turned my face to her so Frank couldn't see me. I mouthed, "Noooo."

Stephanie realized that she couldn't keep a secret (it must run in the family), so she turned to the woman who sat next to her and began to talk.

I looked straight ahead as I tried to avoid Frank's stare.

"Care to share?"

"Share what, boy. Stephanie doesn't know what she's talking about. Plus, she talks too much. You know that," I said as I tried to play it off.

"Naw, I don't know that. C'mon, don't cha want to tell me?" Frank said as he put his index finger into my side.

"Stop, boy, that tickles," I said.

"So, what was your word?" Frank insisted.

"Romans 4:20: '*Abraham staggered not at the promises of God, through unbelief, but was strong in faith, giving God the glory, and being fully persuaded that what God had promised, He was able also to perform.*' " I rattled the Scripture off my tongue.

"*And because of his faithfulness, God declared him righteous*," Frank added as he finished the Scripture for me.

My mouth hung wide open—wide enough for flies, my grandmother would have said.

With his strong hands, Frank rubbed mine with the sweetest of strokes. It was soft, warm, and above all, it was sincere. He felt the excitement that radiated from my body, so he gave me my hand back, passed me my Bible and winked. The service started.

As wonderful as it was to have Stephanie and Frank there with me, I wanted most to hear a word from the Lord through His manservant, Bishop Jones. That was why I put all that I had to do for the week on the back burner. All week long I saw, beheld and soaked in every word, every breath, every moan and groan he made. Bishop stood erect as his stature commanded my attention. His voice rang through me with assurance and with direction. His physical characteristics didn't matter to me. Instead, I saw him in a different light. I saw him as a man who was called with greatness in mind. He was a man who loved God with his whole heart and spoke from its depth. His words exuded strength and assurance in the God he served. When I heard him speak God's Word with such passion and force, I shouted, "Hallelujah," before it even entered my mind to do so. Oh, I was glad to be there.

I longed for the Word. I longed to be in the presence of Jesus and His anointing. I just wanted a little bit of *it* to fall on me, and as it looked in the auditorium, a whole lot of people wanted *it,* too. People of different shapes, sizes and colors packed the center. Men came dressed in suits, jeans and work uniforms. Women were everywhere, dressed in everything from their Sunday-morning best, to jeans and sweats. Like I said, people were everywhere. It was a vast sea of colors. It was God's people gathered together, on one accord, to hear God's manservant speak and proclaim God's Word. It was awesome.

I wish I could retell the sermon. I wish I had the words or insight to retell it. I wish I could give justice to his sermon, but I can't. You just have to take my word for it. The sermon was riveting and passionate. Bishop Jones spoke fluently and swiftly. His words were deliberate and precise. If the Word didn't move you, then it wasn't for you. But as I looked around the huge, lighted auditorium, a lot of folks were moved. A giant praise was lifted up in that place. Mouths moved but were silent. Some stood with their hands raised. Some cried while wet teardrops trickled down their faces. People ran through the stadium as though their feet were on fire and shouted from the top of their lungs, "Praise God, Praise God."

A mighty rush of "Hallelujahs" filled the air. "Glory to God" resounded with a great thunder, and His anointing was there. God's glory was there. GOD was in the hiz-zous. (For us older people, that means "His house." Nicole and Jordan taught me that.) The service was wonderful, awesome, and it blew my mind. The Spirit of God really rained down on us as the night turned spectacular and glorious.

Before the service ended, Bishop asked the congregation to pick a partner to pray with. Frank and I immediately turned to each other. We looked into each other's eyes and froze. It was as if Frank read my thoughts and I his. We bowed our heads in submission to God, and I prayed first. I thanked God for our relationship—a relationship built on trust and friendship, a relationship that was based on God's Word and His commandments and a relationship of celibacy. Frank prayed and prayed and gave God the glory for the things He had done in our lives. We said, "Amen," and hugged one another. Frank gave the best hugs in the world. His arms engulfed me. He wrapped me in security and warmth. His hugs were filled with sincerity and love. As Frank held me in his arms he whispered, "Did I tell you how much I love you today?"

I stepped back and said, "No," with a grin.

"Well, I do love you," Frank said seriously. His eyes deepened.

Something down on the inside of me quickened in my spirit. I looked around at the sight of people as they praised and worshipped God from their hearts. It was so powerful. "Do you love me *this* much?" I asked Frank as I opened my arms far apart. I tried to capture the size of the auditorium in the width of space between my hands.

Frank turned me around so I faced him and said, "How's this?"

He paused. Peace reigned through my spirit as I stood there looking at him. Frank took something out of his pocket, placed it in my hand and said, "Will you marry me?"

Time stood still. Without a thought, I pulled Frank close to me. It was as if those thousands of people who were there a second before had disappeared. I didn't say anything at first; I just hugged him. Then, I whispered in his ear, "I would be honored to marry you."

Frank hugged me tight. What I felt that moment would forever be in my memory. I didn't really cry, cry. I was still in shock. Frank tried to let go of me, but I wouldn't let him. I couldn't believe it. I could not believe Frank proposed.

In my head, I went over and over his words to me. Did he say what I think he said? Naw, naw, he didn't just propose marriage, did he?

Frank pulled us apart, looked me in my eyes and asked me to open the square-shaped box I had cupped in my hand. I said, "No, I'm not opening it."

That moment was too REAL. The moment I had dreamed and prayed for had finally happened. Frank took the box out of my hand and opened it for me.

It was as if a thousand of the brightest flashes of light went off at the same time. The ring's glow was glorious, spectacular and incredible. Man, did it sparkle. It was just absolutely, positively gorgeous. It was a diamond ring. And, it wasn't a little tiny stone either; brother bought a rock. I immediately thought about Matthew 16:18-19. It said, "...*upon this rock I will build My church; and the very gates of hell shall not prevail against it. And I will give unto thee the keys of the kingdom of heaven; and whatsoever thou shalt bind on earth shall be bound in heaven; and whatsoever thou shalt loose on earth shall be loosed in heaven.*"

Frank then took my hand, which might I add, was as calm as the sea (after the storm) the Lord walked on. Anyway. He took my hand and placed the ring upon my finger. I stared at it in amazement and in awe. Not because of its size or its clarity, but I was in awe of GOD—how brightly His Word, His deeds, His blessings shined so miraculously in my life.

I looked around me and saw miracles as they happened right before my eyes. I saw two men in particular. They ran around the auditorium in opposite directions with their eyes closed. As they approached each other at full speed, (I braced myself for the collision) they passed each other without incident. No boom, no brush of the shoulders, nothing. That, was God.

After I praised God for His Word and my marriage proposal,

I tapped Stephanie on her shoulder. She had witnessed the two men as well.

"Did you see that?" she asked.

"No, did you see this?" I said.

I looked down at my hand. She followed my lead. I extended my hand and the lights from the ceiling struck the ring just right. Stephanie stepped back at first; then she looked at me and tears fell from her eyes. She hugged me quickly and then started her own thing. Stephanie shouted like I had never seen before. Her feet moved. Her hands waved. Her mouth opened and praises to God flowed. My heart raced with gladness as I saw her praise God. I looked back to see Frank's reaction, and he had the sweetest and cutest smile on his face I had ever seen. I looked at him and said to myself, "This is MY man God has chosen for me." Then, I had to praise God some more.

Exhausted, Frank and I sat in the car before we headed home. "Frank," I said, "why did you propose to me in church?"

"It was the perfect place," he said without any doubt. "I thought about proposing at the beach, but when you invited me to church, I knew right then, that's where I'd do it."

"God is so good," I yelled as I explained to Frank that it was a secret desire of mine to be proposed to in church. I felt that whoever was to be my husband had to recognize that God was first in my life. And a proposal in church meant that person understood and accepted God's role in my life. I told him that no other person in the world knew my desire other than God. God knew my deepest desire and granted it to me.

"When do you want to get married?" I asked.

Frank then said to me, "I don't have any plans tomorrow."

I looked at him like he had lost his mind. "Dear, that's too soon for me," I said laughing. I wanted a church wedding with a gown, veil and the works. So I needed a bit more time to plan our wedding properly. Immediately, God spoke to my spirit, "July first."

I jumped up in my seat and startled Frank.

"What? What's wrong?" he asked.

"July first, that's the date," I said to Frank.

"One July it is," Frank said in his military talk.

With Frank's cell phone, I called my momma. It was almost midnight, but I didn't care. I was so excited. I had to tell her, and I didn't want to wait until the morning. The timing of Frank's proposal could have not been better. I had just asked my momma a few days before to go with me as I looked for wedding gowns. She thought I was crazy.

"Moniqué, has the boy asked you to marry him?" Momma asked.

"No, Momma. But it won't kill you to go with me anyway," I remembered saying to her.

Momma reluctantly went with me. As we drove to the bridal shop, I told her, "Momma, I know he hasn't proposed, but when he does, I want to be ready."

"And when is the wedding?" she said with a this-fool-is-crazy look. "It don't matter, whatever you say, I'ma circle it all right, in pencil," she said as she taunted me.

I remembered secretly rolling my eyes at her. She didn't see me, though.

So, I *had* to call Momma first.

~~~~~~~~~

Frank and I went to breakfast, and afterwards he dropped me off at my apartment. It was almost two in the morning, but the hour didn't prevent me as I called everyone I knew. After Momma, Darren was first on the list. Darren simply said that he knew that this moment would come some day. He just didn't think it would be that soon. Then, I called almost everyone in my phone book. Yes, at two in the morning. I eventually ran out of people to call.

I sat on the bed and reached for my Bible. I turned again to Romans and read chapter four. By that point, I had read and reread the Scripture so many times during that week, I knew it by heart. All week long I had studied and meditated on it. I said and believed that Scripture *waaay* down in my spirit. I believed that I had staggered not and was sure, was strong in my faith, giving careful detail to give God the glory for the wonderful things He had done in my life.

Eventually, I fell asleep around five in the morning, but not before I thanked God once again for His miracles.

~~~~~~~~

"Darren!" I said, shocked to see him at my door that early in the morning. I had just gone to sleep.

Darren paced my living room and spoke barely above a whisper. His mood was serious, and I was still half-asleep.

I stood at the door and leaned into it. I really didn't know what to do or what to say.

"I just have three questions to ask you."

"Okay," I said.

"Do you love him?"

"Yes, I really do."

242

"Is he a good man?" Darren asked.

"Yeah, he is."

"And my last question. Will you allow him to take my place in the kids' lives?"

"Never."

Tears streamed down my face as I hugged Darren as tight as I could.

## CHAPTER TWENTY-EIGHT

The last couple of months had been a blur with all the things that had to be planned, prepared and put into place for our wedding. But we worked it out. Frank and I had decided early on what we wanted our ceremony to be like. It would be small, family-oriented. Frank was in charge of the honeymoon. I was in charge of everything that dealt with the church ceremony. And Momma had the details of the reception. The wedding party was simple; Frank's groomsmen were Charles and Jordan and my maid of honor was Nicole. That's all we needed to become a family. I was blessed to find a gown I liked at the first place I shopped. It was off-white with lace, form-fitting and it had a long train. I loved it from the moment I tried it on. Everything we needed was supplied. It was a miracle. A few weeks before the ceremony, I mailed out our invitations.

*Moniqué Clark Kennedy*
*and*
*Mr. Frank R. Thompson, IV*
*Request the honor of your presence*
*As they enter the Holy State of Matrimony*

*on*
*July first*
*3:00 p.m.*
*"What God has joined together, Let no man put asunder."*

~~~~~~~~

*"Payment expected at time of service"* was the sign I read on the clinic wall that specialized in HIV/AIDS testing. I placed my name on the waiting list and sat down. I chose the clinic because I wanted anonymity. The room was filled with people of all types of ethnic and age groups. I couldn't believe the number of people that were in the room. At home, I casually listened to the reports on the nightly news, but being in the clinic, seeing the faces, made it oh, so real. Most of the faces there were solemn, expressionless. And the few, like me, who managed a smile, faked it just like I did. A poster on the wall read, "Daily, of the five hundred people who will contract the HIV/AIDS virus, only *one* in five hundred will *know* that they have it…Get tested today!" My heart raced, especially when I heard my name called so quickly. I literally jumped out of my seat.

I walked slowly behind the lady dressed in a multicolored smock. We passed room after room.

"Ma'am, can I get you to stand over by the door for a second. I need to go back up front for a minute."

"Sure," I said as I leaned against the off-white walls.

I heard deep sobs coming from a door, which was slightly ajar. Curiosity got the better of me as I purposely peered inside. There was a man dressed in a deep green Armani suit and snake-skinned shoes. He was lying on his back with both of his hands

246

covering his eyes, crying. Right by his side sat an elegant looking woman who wept softly, holding on to his bed. I heard him tell her, "I'm so sorry. It's all my fault."

"Ma'am, Ma'am. I really need you to follow me," the nurse insisted as she shook her head at me.

Closing the door to my room behind us, the nurse placed the manilla folder on the small desk. She walked over to the cabinet and reached for the syringe, cotton swabs, alcohol wipes and a label. She printed my name legibly, in slow motion.

"Why are you here today?"

It was so hard for me to answer her. My reason for being there was so complicated. This particular period in my life had been the happiest in years, but yet, that moment reminded me of some of the lowest times in my life.

"I need to be tested for AIDS." My voice trembled with each syllable.

"Do you have reason to believe you've been infected?" she asked.

My mind went immediately to Greg and the STD I got from him. I definitely had placed myself in a good position to have the virus numerous times. But before I could answer, we heard a deafening shriek.

The nurse opened the door and said, "I'll be right back."

The wait only intensified the moment even the more. Although I knew that God had forgiven me of my past sins, I also knew that my sins had consequences.

"We can continue now," were her words as she entered the room and began rolling up my shirtsleeve. She studied the bulging veins in my left arm as she placed her sterile gloves on her own hands. Tying the plastic tourniquet around my arm in a tight knot, she pushed the needle into my skin. I closed my eyes. It didn't hurt. I just didn't want to see the blood.

"You know we are the ones getting this disease, don't you?" she said as the blood flowed into the tube.

My eyes concentrated on her lips.

"For some reason, women think they are immune somehow to this disease. There are two things that protect you from the AIDS virus, abstinence or a latex condom, used regularly and correctly every time you have sex. And from what I've seen on a daily basis, condoms ain't full proof."

With my blood safely stored in the small tube, the nurse folded my arm like a lawn chair. "Hold that in place for a few," she said pointing to the crimson-stained cotton swab. She walked over to the desk and completed the paperwork in the file. I heard her mumble to herself, "We don't insist on a condom because we are so in love with them, when, in reality, we should be so in love with ourselves, our life." She turned her attention back to me, "How do you want to be notified, Ma'am?"

"Excuse me?"

"Notified. How do you want your test results? Phone, mail…"

"I can't get them today?" I hollered, not realizing it.

The nurse took two steps backward before speaking. "Honey, you didn't give me a chance to finish." She looked at me so she could continue talking. "Or you can wait like the others out in the lobby. We will call you when we get the results."

"How long does it normally take, the results, I mean?"

"You're here early, so it shouldn't take long." She ushered me out of the room, gave me a number and walked me down the hall toward the waiting area. The walls were lined with posters from the Center for Disease Control that I didn't remember being there before. The first one I read blew my mind:

- A Black woman is 23 times more likely to be infected with the AIDS-causing HIV virus. The phenomenon, appears to stem from these women having sex with Black men who—while not labeling themselves as gay or bisexual—have unprotected sex with other men behind their wives' and girlfriends' backs. The CDC has called Black bisexual males the "bridge" between gay men and heterosexual women. A recent research study has suggested that as many as 30 percent of Black bisexual men may be HIV-infected. Worse, up to 90 percent of these men don't know they're carrying the virus.

"Ninety percent." I said aloud.

The nurse shook her head yes, as I read more facts posted on the walls.

- At issue for Black women are their lifestyle choices.
- Some 67 percent of Black women with HIV/AIDS contracted the virus through heterosexual sex. Today Black women make up more than half of all women who have died of AIDS.
- AIDS is claiming and destroying the lives of millions of people of all ethnic groups. We need to be wise and informed about HIV, AIDS, and STDs for our own sakes and for those we care about.
- If you or your partner can't or won't discuss safe sex, then you should not have sex with that person. After all, it is *your* health and life at risk.

"Honey, at this rate, you will never get to the waiting room. Here, take this pamphlet; it has all this information and much more. And if you have access to the Internet, just type in the search engine, *women AIDS*," the nurse said as I stared at the posters with my mouth wide open.

We reached the waiting room as all eyes widened at the sight of the nurse with a manilla folder in her hand. As she walked away, the heavy sighs in the room could be heard like thunder.

As soon as I sat down to open the pamphlet, my cell phone rang.

"Hello." I tried to sound as upbeat as I could.

"Hey, you. How's my love today?" Frank asked.

"I'm fine. And you?"

"Are you okay? There's something not right in your voice. Hey, we're getting married next week; you're supposed to be happy."

I wanted to drop the phone. Would he still marry me if the results were positive? Would he stick around, out of pity?

"Dear? You there?" Frank's voice was alarmed.

"Frank, I'm here. Actually, I'm at the clinic, getting my AIDS test done like we talked about."

"You sound a little worried," Frank said.

"Exactly." I got up and stepped outside the clinic's front door. Putting on my dark sunglasses, I took in the early morning sunlight.

Compassionate as ever, Frank said, "Moniqué Clark Kennedy. I love you, girl." Frank paused, "And the rest, we will figure out if need be. Moniqué, did you hear me?"

"Yeah," I said watching all the cars entering and exiting the parking lot.

"I was scared, too, dear, when I took my test the other day. It's amazing the stuff you remember when in that situation. Stuff you try to bury real deep. But I tell you what, when I got that negative result back, I shouted and praised God like I had lost my mind. I know you remember, because I called you."

Just then, the door swung open and a small lady said to me, "Are you number eight?"

I looked down at the crumpled piece of paper in my hand and unrolled it. In bold black print it read, *eight*.

"Frank, I gotta go. They just called my number. I promise to call you with the results, okay?"

"All right. Try not to worry."

Before entering the building, I took a long deep breath and said a prayer, "Your will be done God. In Jesus's name, Amen."

"Honey, you better get in here, I don't think they're going to call your number again," the concerned lady said.

I turned around and went in.

Five minutes later, I walked out to the car with my head down, shaking it. Opening the door, I sat and placed my head against the steering wheel, hitting the sides of it with my hands. The piece of paper with the results on it floated like a feather to the floor. Tears streamed down my face faster than I could wipe them off. I picked up the results off the floor and called Frank on my cell. He answered on the first ring.

"It's negative," I hollered. I opened my mouth and shouted at the top of my lungs, "Thank You, Jesus! For Your grace and mercy endure forever."

## CHAPTER TWENTY-NINE

The morning of my wedding, I wrote in my journal:

*Lord God, when no one else loved me, You did. When no one else cared, You did. When I laid on my face in the midnight hour, Lord, You held me in Your arms and rocked me to sleep. It is You, Holy Spirit, who grants me peace and joy—joy that resides in my bosom. Lord, it was only You who granted me a second chance at love, a second chance for happiness. I know that marriage takes a lot of hard work, commitment and stick-to-it-ness. I know it's more compromise than satisfaction. I know you have to give more than you receive. But most of all, it's about honoring and worshipping You as a couple. Giving YOU, Lord, Your props. Giving You the praise, in season and out of season. Lord, I thank You for giving me a mate that when we kneel down in prayer, we will be on one accord, that where two people are gathered in Your name and touch and agree, You will be in the midst. Thank You, Father, for being in the midst. Thank You, Lord, for walking and talking with us. Lord, thank You for making us one in Christ Jesus, our Savior.*

*Again, Lord, You have made me laugh. But I also thank You for the many tears I have shed and will shed, because it was those crying and hurting times that got me to this point, my wedding day.*

*Lord, I thank You in advance for the things You are about to do through Frank and myself. Thank You for allowing us to share in Your kingdom. Thank You, Jesus, for allowing us to walk the path that You have set for us. Thank You, Lord. Truly, I thank You. I am so grateful to You. Thank You for the smile, Lord. You know what it's for. It's only through Your grace, mercy and love that I smile on today. I smile, I stand, I sing, I wave my hands to You. I lift up my voice in a happy song on today, because when the enemy thought he had ME, I got away. Hallelujah.*

*Jesus Christ, my LORD, I can't thank You enough. All of those times I fell for those shallow lies. Lies of everlasting and undying love. Lies of deceit and of deception. When I didn't or couldn't believe in myself. When I thought I had no place to turn to. When I would lie awake in my bed but could not sleep. When I would get in my car, but had no place to go. When I called a friend and the line would just ring and ring. When I had no money to pay the bills. When the food got low and I had no gas in the car. When checks bounced. When so-called friends turned away. When I had no one to hold me. No one to really love me. When I had given up, thrown in the towel. When I no longer wanted to live but did not have the nerve to die. When, when, when Lord, when I had nowhere to turn to. YOU WERE THERE. You did not give up on me. You did not turn me away. You just sat there and loved me. You touched me. You caressed me. You told me that I was special and loved by You. You said that I belonged to You. You said so. HALLELUJAH.*

*So this day, Heavenly Father, July first, is dedicated to YOU. To Your awesome power of resurrection and of hope. This day is Yours. It is the manifestation of Your glory. It will prove once again to the world that You live. That when the world says no, You say yes. When the world is busy getting divorced, You say marriage. When the world yells at the top of its lungs hate, You tell us all to Love. So this day and every day of my life is dedicated to YOU.*

## CHAPTER THIRTY

I wasn't nervous at all that day. As I tapped my foot against the tiled floor, I wanted to get the show on the road. If anything, I was anxious. Not so much for the wedding night, but to become Mrs. Frank R. Thompson, IV. It was my name, and it was who God had chosen me to be. I wanted it; it was mine. God meant it for me, and no other woman in this entire world could claim him. He wasn't theirs to have. He was mine. I guess I got a little carried away with myself. Anyway. It was three o'clock in the afternoon and Frank and I were ready to be married. I heard the music as it played while I sat alone in the kitchen of New Hope Baptist Church. It was the same church where I had ushered, sang in the choir and was baptized. It was also the same church I first got saved in. And on that day, it would be the same church where I would be married.

Shaun entered the sanctuary first and took his place at the center of the altar. Frank and Charles followed as they wore their matching black and white tuxedos. Frank stepped to the altar as Charles walked right into him. The congregation laughed and Charles, embarrassed, buried his head in the back of Frank's tuxedo to hide his face. Frank kept pulling Charles from behind

257

him, but every time he did that, Charles hid behind Frank more.

Jordan walked through the door of the parlor where I sat, looked at me and simply said, "Come on."

"Come on?" I thought as I looked at him.

For the first time in his life, Jordan was in charge of his momma, and he liked it. He grabbed my hand and walked me out to the vestibule area where I saw Linda. She smiled from ear to ear. *You are so beautiful*, by Babyface, played in the background. Two ushers stood at the doors to the entrance of the sanctuary. When I got close to one of them, he whispered in my ear, "You're glowing, Moniqué."

I blushed. I looked down at Jordan who had extended his arm to me and said, "Are you ready?"

"Yep," he said.

Nicole had already made her solo entrance into the sanctuary. From what I heard, Nicole was a mini-me.

The doors opened to the invited onlookers. I heard several gasps as they stood to their feet. Lights flashed before my eyes.

Jordan walked to the edge of the first pew and stopped. I took one step forward and paused before I joined him. As I did, Jordan bowed, I curtsied, then he wrapped my hand around his little arm. Jordan walked proudly beside me down the rose-petaled aisle.

As I walked down the aisle, I saw all of my friends and former co-workers. I saw people I had known for years, people who knew me when I was a little girl. Everyone was there, and it felt just wonderful. People blew kisses and winked at me. There wasn't a dry eye in the house. I couldn't believe it. I approached the altar and saw Frank's family and mine. All of them looked like they were at a dentist convention. They were all teeth. I felt a bit

258

sentimental and needed some added strength. So I looked at Stephanie and Regina for the extra boost to my spirit. NOT. Those jokers sat next to each other and cried like hungry twins. You'd thought I had died instead of the fact that I was getting married. As a last ditched effort, I looked at Shaun. He would be a pillar of strength, right? Wrong. I had no one to look at, but Frank. And I knew, if I looked at him, I would just lose it. I looked anyway.

Oh, he looked so wonderful. So elegant and handsome. He was F-F-Fine. (No, my baby was better than that.) He was a prayer realized. He looked at me as if I was the only woman in the sanctuary. Nothing else or no one mattered at that moment. Frank didn't take his eyes off me. I couldn't take my eyes off of him. I smiled and he returned the same.

We stood there at the altar in front of God, our children, family and friends.

" *'They that wait upon the Lord shall renew their strength, They shall mount up on wings of eagles, They shall run and not be weary and They shall walk and not faint.'* Let the church say Amen," Shaun instructed.

"Amen," the congregation shouted.

"You may be seated," Shaun said as the congregation sat.

"Let me first state that this is a worship experience. A celebration. I'm conscious of the fact that we have come primarily to worship God and to honor what God has chosen to do in the coming together of Frank and Moniqué. God be praised for this privilege.

"My dear friends, we are gathered here to celebrate what God has decided. He determined that Frank and Moniqué will declare their love. We do not take this moment lightly, as you stand before me and ultimately before God," Shaun admonished us.

Shaun looked in Jordan's direction and said, "Who gives this beautiful Black woman to this strong Black man?"

Jordan let go of my hand and said, "I do."

The entire congregation laughed and clapped in response to Jordan's young voice. Shaun laughed, too. Jordan placed my hand in Frank's and stood beside Charles. I squeezed Frank's hand, twice.

"I've done a lot of weddings, and never has that statement gotten a handclap," Shaun remarked as he continued the ceremony. "I'm not foolish enough to think love is always so peaceful. Most folk won't admit, but you two are mature, that there is conflict, confusion and crisis in our relationships." Shaun looked at the congregation and then back at Frank and me. "If God has brought you together and you both believe it, in difficult times, that must be what keeps you together, because if you ever lose sight of the fact that your relationship is transcendent in origin, then you will lose the will of God, which is the safest place to be."

Frank and I kept our eyes on Shaun.

"You both told me that not only do you love one another but that you love God and you honestly, firmly believed that God has brought you together. That has to keep you, in everything else, that has to keep you.

"What I want to remind you is that if you start with God, don't decide when it gets good, that God can be second."

Shaun turned his focus to me. "Moniqué, you and I have been through a whole lot of stuff together. Folk in this building wouldn't believe our relationship," Shaun laughed.

He probably remembered all the dumb questions I asked him.

"And one of the things I celebrate with you today, if I can be very honest, is that he's a reminder that God will bless you when you love Him the most," Shaun said as he pointed first to Frank and then to the ceiling.

Tears trickled down my face as Nicole handed me a tissue. I dabbed my face. I didn't want to ruin my makeup.

Shaun focused back on Frank and me.

"Love God. For if you keep loving God, God will give you your heart's desire." Shaun paused after his powerful statement. "And now, we move forward. The question now is, do ya'll still want to do this?" Shaun had a wide smile on his face.

The congregation, Frank and I, and Shaun laughed.

"I suspect that is a yes," Shaun replied.

"Yes," Frank answered.

I turned to Frank.

"So, Frank, will you take Moniqué to be your wife; will you commit yourself to her happiness and self-fulfillment as a person and to her usefulness in the kingdom of God and will you promise to love, honor, trust and serve her in sickness and health, adversity and prosperity, to be true and loyal to her, so long as you both shall live?"

"I will," Frank said as he looked into my eyes.

"Moniqué, will you take Frank to be your husband; will you commit yourself to his happiness and self-fulfillment as a person and to his usefulness in the kingdom of God and will you promise to love, honor, trust and serve him in sickness and health, adversity and prosperity, to be true and loyal to him, so long as you both shall live?"

"I will," I said as I felt like that very moment in time was the very place God wanted for me to be my entire life.

"May I have the rings please?" Shaun took the rings from the ring bearer and looked at them closely. "This is real gold, expensive stuff," Shaun said as he held the rings up for the congregation to see. "My brother, you are a bad boy."

Frank's chest rose about three inches.

"Gold is precious of all the elements, but you know how gold becomes pure? Through fire, pain and disappointment. Your love, above all, should be the most valuable thing you have in the earth. Treat it that way. So, every time you see these rings, it's a reminder of how valuable he is to you and she is to you." Shaun pointed to us. "Let's pray. Father, consecrate now these rings, In Jesus's name, Amen."

We lifted our heads and glanced at each other. Shaun instructed us to repeat after him when it was our turn.

"Moniqué, with this ring, I pledge my life and my love to you, in the name of the Father, the Son and the Holy Spirit, Amen," Frank said as he placed the ring on my left ring finger.

"Frank, with this ring, I pledge my life and my love to you, in the name of the Father, the Son and the Holy Spirit, Amen," I said, as I did the same with Frank's ring.

"Since you two have come together to make this public commitment, with as much joy as I have had in a long time, I now pronounce you husband and wife, man and wo-man, partner and soul mate, for the rest of your natural born lives."

Frank and I stood smiling at Shaun as he continued, "How wonderful God is to give us another opportunity for love. May you go now in the strength of God. May the joy of God rest upon you. May the forgiveness of God live in you. May the agape love of God order your steps. May the Word of God be a constant reminder that God is sovereign. And may everything that you touch prosper. May you never have a day of not knowing that you're loved by the other. And may your love be a symbol of how great

God is, and in fifty years may we do this again."

All that Shaun said was wonderful, but I thought, "I know he's not going to dismiss us without a kiss—*my* kiss."

"I now present to you, Mr. and Mrs. Frank Thompson, IV," Shaun said proudly as he extended his arms.

Apparently, he didn't see the look that was on my face. I was like, "Uh, dude. You're forgetting something here."

"Go in the strength of God and have a great life," he said as he tried to usher us from the altar.

Neither Frank nor I moved. I mouthed to Shaun, "My kiss?"

"Oh, I'm sorry." He read my lips to a tee. His eyes got so big as he laughed.

The congregation laughed, too.

"It was the *woman* that reminded me," Shaun said as he patted Frank on his shoulder and said, "You may be in good shape, my brother."

We all laughed at that point.

"Frank, you may, now, salute your bride."

Frank paused for a moment as he held my face in both of his hands. I closed my eyes as I felt the warmth of his lips touch mine. For a brief moment, everyone disappeared except him and me. Our hearts fused together. Our minds were one. Our dreams, our prayers were fulfilled. And God, I felt with everything that was in me, was overjoyed.

Then I heard Stephanie say, "Yeah."

Frank released his grasp of my face and held my hand.

Shaun ushered us out as he said, "Go, go."

As we exited the sanctuary, everyone applauded. And God reminded me of His Word, "All that the Lord has promised...He *will* do."

## CHAPTER THIRTY-ONE

Wwe arrived at our hotel. Frank let me off at the door and parked the car. I waited for him at the front desk. Frank checked us in as the bellman carried our bags to our room. Frank tipped him and closed the door. I sat on the bed and took off my shoes. My feet ached. Frank took one step toward me and said, "Oh, no. I forgot something."

"What?"

Frank turned around and walked to the door, opened it and then closed it again. I'm tempted to tell the rest of the story, but God didn't tell me to share everything. Some things should be kept a secret. I will tell you this...The sign on the door read, "DO NOT DISTURB."

Let it be stated, for the record...IT was worth the wait. (Somebody, Anybody, Everybody...Shout Hallelujah.)

## ABOUT THE AUTHOR

Monique Jewell Anderson is a native of Chesapeake, Virginia, where she lives with her husband, Frank, and their five children who range in age from college to kindergarten. Mrs. Anderson is an avid reader and devout Christian. She will be touring nationwide and speaking extensively on women's issues and the love of Jesus Christ. Her goal is to encourage others and to lift up the name of Jesus Christ wherever she goes. *Plum Crazzzy* is the first in a series of new books by Mrs. Anderson.

# Plum Crazzzy
## Book Club/Reader Questions

## BOOK CLUB/READER QUESTIONS

1. Describe the different qualities and characteristics of the major characters? Which scenes or characters do you relate the most to and why? Which qualities and characteristics are consistent with God's Holy Word and which are not?

2. What lessons did you learn from Moniqué?

3. Why did the main character, Moniqué, keep seeing Mark after the first betrayal? Have you ever continued a relationship after a betrayal? Why? What has been the result?

4. At what point in your life is your past your past? When entering a new relationship, what do you reveal about yourself and why?

5. Should Mark have stepped down from his position in the church? And if so, at what point should he have done so? Are people in church positions held to a higher standard? Should they be?

6. Do you think Moniqué's character is representative of most women or are her character traits and experiences specific to women of a particular race, socio-economic background and/or religious perspective?

7. Are you at risk of acquiring a sexually transmitted disease? What are you doing to minimize your risk? Do you know if your partner has an STD? How do you know?

8. Why does Moniqué continue to attract the "misfit man" and how does she "change her scent"?

9. Do you need forgiveness or healing? Do you need to forgive anyone? What is the importance of forgiveness in Moniqué's relationship with God and with others?

10. Have you accepted Jesus Christ as your Lord and Savior? How do you know? What does it mean to be saved?

# Biblical Scriptures for Meditation and Study

## Selected Scriptures for Meditation and Study

**Psalm 51:10**, Create in me a clean heart, O God; and renew a right spirit within me.

**Psalm 30:5b**, Weeping may endure for a night, but joy comes in the morning.

**Proverbs 1:7**, The fear of the LORD is the beginning of knowledge, but fools despise wisdom and instruction.

**John 3:16**, For God so loved the world, that He gave His only begotten Son, that whoever believes in Him should not perish, but have everlasting life.

**Joshua 1:9**, Have I not commanded you? Be strong and of good courage; do not be afraid, nor dismayed, for the LORD your God is with you wherever you go.

**Romans 5:8**, But God demonstrates His love toward us, in that while we were still sinners, Christ died for us.

**Romans 6:23**, For the wages of sin is death, but the gift of God is eternal life through Christ Jesus our Lord.

**John 6:28, 29**, They replied, "What does God want us to do?" Jesus told them, "This is what God wants you to do; Believe in the One He has sent."

**1 John 1:9**, But if we confess our sins to Him, He is faithful and just to forgive us and to cleanse us from every wrong.

**Matthew 4:17**, From that time on Jesus began to preach, "Repent, for the kingdom of heaven is near."

# ADDITIONAL GREAT TITLES
## FROM
# LITERALLY SPEAKING PUBLISHING HOUSE

# THREE NATIONAL BESTSELLERS IN A ROW

*CHOCOLATE THOUGHTS*
*MOCHA LOVE*
*BLESSED ASSURANCE*

ADDITIONAL GREAT TITLES
from
LITERALLY SPEAKING PUBLISHING HOUSE
Available in Bookstores Nationwide

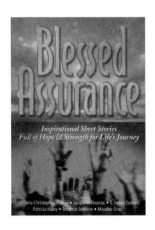

S. JAMES GUITARD, VICTORIA CHRISTOPHER MURRAY, JACQUELIN
THOMAS, PATRICIA HALEY, MAURICE GRAY
AND TERRANCE JOHNSON

With all of the chaos, confusion, and uncertainty of life, we all need to know of the blessed assurances that God has for our lives. Fast-paced, witty, entertaining, and inspirational, the writings in *Blessed Assuranc*e are modern day renditions of biblical stories. A national bestseller, *Blessed Assurance* is an enjoyable, empowering, engaging, and encouraging example of the everlasting truth that God can move us from heartache to healing, burden to blessings, depression to deliverance, and from trials to triumphs.

In the short story, *The Best of Everything*, based on Hannah, you gain a better level of appreciation and thankfulness for what

God has already done in your life, which will provide you with strength to endure in the midst of a crisis as well as give you patience as you await new blessings. *Lust and Lies*, based on Samson and Delilah, reminds us of the temptations of lust, the importance of honesty, the dangers of sin and the significance of repentance. *Traveling Mercies*, based on the parable of the Good Samaritan, teaches us not to place limitations on how and through whom God may send a blessing, and our responsibility to help people whom we often do not know.

*Baby Blues*, based on Abraham and Sarah, lets us better understand the importance of timing, patience, and the consequences of operating in God's permissive will versus God's perfect will for our lives. *A Sprig of Hope*, based on Tamar, acknowledges that tragedy, sadness and betrayal are an unfortunate part of life, and yet ultimately there is healing, restoration and happiness if you place your trust in God. *Sword of the Lord*, based on Jephthah, confirms that your past can't define you if you give your future to God and that everyone at some time or another needs to forgive as well as receive forgiveness.

ISBN: 1929642-12-1          Format: Hardcover
Retail Price: $19.95